DELPHINIUMS AND DECEPTION

DIANA FLOWERS FLORICULTURE MYSTERIES

RUBY LOREN

BRITISH AUTHOR

Please note, this book is written in British English and contains British spellings.

BOOKS IN THE SERIES

1

RETREAT

The delphiniums had started their final flush when Fergus Robinson knocked on my door. It was only when I saw his perpetually thoughtful face, tanned by the sun of the summer, that I realised we hadn't seen each other for months. After all of the neighbourhood drama at my old house, I'd finally accepted that the cottage and land I'd been left in a will wasn't the perfect place for my cut flower business after all. I'd made it through the first summer there, but as soon as autumn had shown its colours, I'd completed the sale of the property and moved into a new house and land that Fergus had placed on my radar.

The last owner of my new property had been emigrating to Spain that very winter and all had worked out for the better. I'd even had help cultivating my first flower field. Fergus had been very eager to do some digging on my new land. Sure, I knew it was because he'd been looking for a solid gold coffin and the roman vampire that may or may not be inside, but I'd appreciated his help all the same - even when Dracula had never materialised.

In the time that had followed the hard work of the

1

RUBY LOREN

autumn and winter, my business had very literally begun to blossom. I'd feared that, with the village gossip being what it was, being tangled up in the shocking events at Little Larchley could damage my business. The locals regularly shunned anyone who was perceived to have caused trouble. Rocking the boat was not the done thing in Merryfield. But when spring sprung, and I finally had enough flowers and greenery to attend the local markets again, I'd been surprised to find that the exact opposite had happened. The locals had flocked to my flower stall to find out every last detail about the sordid history of Little Larchley. And while they'd listened to me answer their questions, a lot of them had bought flowers.

The summer that had followed was my best yet. The florists I'd pitched my business to had all increased their standing orders, and I'd also supplied flowers for several events. The article in a national newspaper that had shouted about the benefits of purchasing British-grown flowers, and handily featured an interview with little old me, hadn't exactly hurt matters either. The money I'd sacrificed by upping sticks from my first premises was more than recouped, and I was proud to say that *Diana Flowers Blooms* looked as though it was here to stay. It had been more than a year since I'd left my job working as a chemical analyst, and it was still the best decision I had ever made.

"Fergus! It's so nice to see you," I said, opening the door and simultaneously trying to smooth my auburn hair. I wasn't particularly fussy about my appearance, but I'd spent the morning deadheading some of the final late summer blooms, and I strongly suspected I looked like I'd waltzed through a hedge backwards. My dog, Diggory, surged past my legs, nearly sending me flying in his eagerness to see Fergus. The man on my doorstep bent to ruffle Diggory's hairy brown ears and laughed when the canine comically looked past him and then questioningly up at him.

"Sorry. Barkimedes is at the vet," he told the disappointed dog.

"Oh no! Has something happened to him? I hope it's not serious?" Barkimedes was Fergus' dog - a brown and white 'Heinz 57' breed (much like Diggory was!) who had become firm friends with my dog.

Fergus pulled a face. "That depends on who you ask. I personally think that eating an artifact which could have had some huge historical implications is a serious matter, but Barkimedes seemed pretty pleased with himself." He shot me a grin. "He's fine. The vet is just concerned because I told him about some of the electromagnetic influences that the artifact might have been subjected to. He wanted to keep Barkimedes in for observation, in case there were any negative side effects."

I nodded like this statement made complete sense. Fergus was obsessed with conspiracy theories. He spent so much time studying them that I wasn't actually sure what he did in order to make a living. The conspiracy-themed website named 'The Truth Beneath' had written that his work had something to do with a security service, but I still had yet to be enlightened as to what, exactly, that meant. Somehow, Fergus had managed to dodge every question I'd ever asked on that front.

"How's business?" Fergus asked, shoving his hands into the pockets of his jeans and looking pensively across at my flower field and polytunnels.

"It's going very well, if you don't count the distinct lack of mysterious items buried on this property," I told him with a smile, knowing exactly what he was getting at with his casual question. "You never know. There's a whole field still to cultivate. Perhaps we'll find that roman vampire next sowing season."

Fergus shrugged. "You can keep your vampire. I'm just interested in the solid gold coffin." He shook his head as though I was the crazy one.

I reached out and jabbed his arm. "Are you coming in for tea?"

"Am I invited?" Fergus joked back. I found myself grinning as our friendship slotted back into place the way it had ever since Fergus' nasty habit of trespassing had brought us together and our shared experiences had made us friends.

"Since when has something as trivial as being invited ever mattered to you?" I jibed before ushering him into my house.

Fergus let out a long, low whistle. "You've been busy since I last came round."

I nodded, quietly proud of what I'd managed to achieve with the old place. If Jim Holmes' bequest had been my training wheels, they'd definitely been removed in this house. It didn't hurt that I'd sold Jim's cottage and land at a higher price than I'd bought this place for, which had allowed me to make purchases for quality's sake rather than price. The difference had come both from the work I'd already done to Jim's old cottage and the fact that the old place had been situated in a hamlet (albeit one with a dicey past). My new house was still relatively close to Merryfield, but it was out in the sticks. According to the estate agent, people didn't like being out in the middle of nowhere without any near neighbours. It would appear that I was an oddity.

"Tartan! So fancy," Fergus said, stroking my relatively new upholstery.

I frowned, knowing that the compliments had turned into lighthearted mockery. "It's cosy!" I protested and then went off to make the tea, not forgetting to put out a plate of biscuits. I'd kept a few unopened packets in the cupboard in case of an unexpected visitor. Truly, I knew I'd had Fergus in mind. According to him, tea wasn't tea without a decent biscuit selection.

I liked to imagine that Fergus wouldn't be my only visitor, but I knew he was the only one who seemed able to spare the time and effort... and the only one who thought it was acceptable to just turn up out of the blue. My best friend, Heather, was busy with her B&B business, and I didn't blame her for not finding a spare moment to chit-chat.

The remainder of my other old school friends no longer had much in common with me. They commuted to the city every day, as I had once done myself. Beyond the past, I'd discovered we had nothing to share with one another. Finally, there were my parents. My mum had come round when I'd deemed the property suitable for showing to family and my father and his new wife had visited, too. Since then, mum had gone off on a six month cruise, as was her custom whenever she could afford it, and my dad was simply scatter-brained enough that he'd probably forgotten how long it had been since we'd last seen one another.

I knew I wasn't blameless either. Days and weeks had turned into months without me realising, and I was certain that anyone sane would advise me to slow down a little when it came to the business. The problem was, it was something that I loved to do. Why would I ever want to slow down?

"Here's your tea," I said, walking out of the kitchen a couple of minutes later. Fergus had installed himself on the tartan sofa he'd critiqued and Diggory had curled up next to him with his head in Fergus' lap.

"He's not allowed on the sofa," I informed my visitor. I actually had reservations about whether or not Fergus should be allowed on there. Both dog and man turned and looked at me with puppy dog eyes. I dumped the tea and biscuits on the coffee table and threw my hands up in defeat.

What was a little extra dog hair to clean in the grand scheme of things?

"So… have you managed to find any evidence to support one of your theories yet?" I asked, knowing I was baiting Fergus, but still feeling annoyed about the tartan comment.

"The evidence is all around us. You just have to know how and where to look," my visitor replied with an air of smugness that made me want to throw one of my also-tartan cushions at him. The only thing that stopped me was the knowledge that tea would be a lot harder to remove from the sofa than dog hair.

Fergus grinned, knowing full well that he was being sanctimonious. "There haven't been any major breakthroughs, unfortunately. However, we did uncover a site of archaeological interest that contained enough historical items of value that the finders' fee will keep us all in business for another year or so." His forehead wrinkled. "Well… it will keep us in business when I finally get one of the more valuable items back from Barkimedes' stomach. It adds something to the item's history though, don't you think?"

I ignored the rather disgusting comment and wondered if I finally had my answer as to how Fergus managed to spend so much time chasing hearsay. Perhaps some of his conspiracy theories genuinely had a grounding in historic truths that directed them to particular sites of interest, only for them to uncover a real piece of history, as opposed to a theoretical one.

Now, that was a conspiracy theory about conspiracy theories that I might actually be willing to entertain!

Fergus took a sip of his tea and then ate two biscuits in a row. I silently cursed that he'd picked the white chocolate zebra biscuits - my favourites. But what kind of host would I be if I hadn't put them out? I congratulated myself on being so selfless. And definitely not begrudging.

"I actually came here to give you your birthday present," he announced in-between devouring the deliciously more-ish morsels.

"My birthday isn't until Saturday," I said, faintly surprised that he'd remembered it at all. Last year I'd mentioned it to him a week before it had occurred. On the day of my birthday, he'd turned up on my doorstep and announced that he'd cooked dinner for us. I'd gone round to his apartment and discovered that his idea of 'dinner' had exploded all over the oven. The evening had ended with us eating takeaway, but it had still been a lot more than I'd planned to do. I'd returned the favour when his birthday had come around in January by cooking him a meal that had actually been edible. We'd still been slaving away in the field back then.

"I know that," Fergus told me. "But it's kind of a once in a lifetime opportunity, so I thought you wouldn't mind if it was early. Get ready to be forever stunned and grateful to me..." he said, building the anticipation. "...We're going on a flower arranging weekend retreat! It's an incredibly exclusive event. Honestly, I'm amazed at myself for managing to get tickets. According to my ticket source, some big influencers in the gardening world will be attending this event." he shrugged. "Not that I'd have any clue about that. But anyway, it's the first course of its kind, and the hype claims it will change the way we arrange flowers forever."

I felt my jaw drop open. "That's fantastic! I've wanted to improve my flower arranging skills since... since forever!" My floriculture had really come on over the past couple of years, but I was still relying on knowledge gleaned from a morning course on flower arranging - that had been run by the Merryfield chapel's flower arrangers - whenever I was forced to stick some flowers in a vase. I knew it was a weak point. "Thank you so much! I don't think anyone's ever got me something so thoughtful before. Didn't it cost a lot? It sounds like something that cost far too much," I fretted.

"Don't worry about it for a moment. I told you - I have contacts."

I nodded, still bowled over by the unexpected gesture. "Then, great! It sounds brilliant. When does the course start? This is so unexpected..." I added, my eyes narrowing for a fraction of a second, before I reprimanded myself for being suspicious. Fergus had always been full of surprises, and this thoughtful gesture must just be another quirk in his personality.

"It starts tomorrow morning! You'd better pack your bags tonight. You didn't have anything planned for your birthday, did you?" Fergus waved a hand. "Trust me - even if you did, it's worth skipping it for this. We are going to have an unforgettable time learning how to arrange some flowers. Yay!" He wiggled his fingers in the air.

I immediately picked up on his use of one worrying little word.

"We?" I queried. Fergus had some pretty varied interests, but I knew for a fact that flowers were not one of them.

"Yep! I'll pick you up tomorrow at eight. See you then!" Fergus got to his feet so suddenly that Diggory fell off the sofa. The three biscuits still remaining on the plate were upended and landed on the new rug I'd bought to cover the rustic reclaimed floorboards. That was all Diggory needed to forgive Fergus' rude wakeup.

"Fergus... what exactly is being taught on this retreat?" I pressed, following him as he beat a suspiciously hasty retreat to the door.

"It's just flower arranging, I swear! But... you know... with a twist." He grinned and then he was gone, trotting down the path back to the safety of his car, where I could ask him no more questions.

"A twist. I should have known," I muttered, wondering just what I was letting myself in for.

My feelings of dread were overcome by the sound of Diggory being sick on my new rug. As far as omens went - not that I gave any credence to something as unscientific as omens - it probably wasn't a good one.

2

LIFE OR DEATH

"I sn't this great?" Fergus said whilst I continued to blink the sleep out of my eyes. I was well-used to early starts, but the lack of clarity about the exact nature of my 'birthday present' had led to a fairly sleepless night. I'd tried to envisage a worst case scenario. Then, I'd attempted to imagine something that would cause Fergus to be interested in an apparent flower arranging course, but I'd drawn a blank.

Until now.

As we drove through the reinforced steel fence - that looked like it was something out of a high security prison rather than the country cottage I'd somehow imagined - I was forced to accept that my imagination hadn't accounted for this. Whatever 'this' turned out to be.

"What's the twist? Are we flower arranging for convicted criminals?" I asked, doubts well and truly setting in.

Fergus hushed me with a wave of his hand. "It really is a flower arranging retreat. I would never lie to you! Just think of it as 'extreme flower arranging'... and that's all I'm going to say."

"Extreme flower arranging?!" I threw Fergus a sharp look of inquiry but he just grinned and mimed zipping his lips shut.

"I'm not even supposed to know that much. It's all top secret. These high-level concept events always are."

I toyed with the idea of sniping about how many high-level events Fergus had actually been to before, but A: I knew that I was just annoyed I'd basically been tricked into coming here, and B: there was still a lot I didn't know about Fergus. Instead, I stayed quiet and was silently glad that at least Diggory hadn't been dragged into whatever the heck this was. Both he and Barkimedes had been dropped off at my dad's house. After being out of contact for the summer, he and Annabelle had been delighted to take the dogs for Fergus and me. Well - Annabelle had been, and my dad - as ever - had agreed with her whilst she'd dropped me a wink and trampled all over his weak protests that a dog would mess up the furniture.

We turned a corner on the long drive that lay beyond the multiple razor wire fences that ringed the strange enclosure we'd driven into. A military style concrete bunker was revealed, sitting in the middle of an otherwise innocuous field with a few trees keeping it company on the flat expanse.

"Wow... this is finally it," Fergus breathed, causing me to shoot him a few extra suspicious looks. My companion may be keeping quiet about why, exactly, he wanted to be on this 'flower arranging' course, but I would get to the bottom of it. Of one thing I was already certain: Fergus had not signed up to learn about flower arranging.

He pulled up outside the bunker and a man dressed in a private security uniform came over and took the keys. "Leave your luggage in the car. It will be unloaded and taken to your rooms," was the only greeting the man offered us.

We watched as he proceeded to drive the Peugeot Partner

van into a garage that appeared when a steel wall slid up and revealed the space behind it. It didn't escape my notice that the other vehicles already in place cost a great deal more than Fergus' beat-up van. Fergus held his hand out for the keys when the security guy acting as a valet walked by, but the man merely shot him a hard-as-nails look.

Fergus withdrew his hand. "I guess you'll give them back later, huh?" He smiled at me to show it was no big deal.

We walked up the slope that led towards what appeared to be the front door of the bunker. Or at least - it was the only door visible.

My conspiracy-minded friend led the way up the final set of steps before the door. I trailed behind, half-wishing I could ask the army/valet guy to bring me a car - any car - so I could get the heck out of here. Fergus had made this whole thing sound like it was something that I'd love, but everything I'd seen so far definitely screamed 'Fergus'. Bunkers, strange car key stealing valets, a mystery course... it was right up the conspiracy theorist's street.

Once through the door, I found myself revising my opinion a little. The exterior had been formed of forbidding blank concrete, but the interior was decked out like a fancy hotel. There was even a reception desk topped with marble and a smiling woman waiting to greet us.

"Are you checking in for the retreat?" she asked, flashing Fergus an even brighter smile that he answered with his own slanting grin. I decided to ignore whatever was going on between the pair.

"We are, yes," I told her before reluctantly looking across at Fergus. He was the one with all of the details.

"Diana Flowers and Fergus Robinson," he told the receptionist. She glanced down at the sheet of paper attached to the clipboard in front of her. Her face visibly fell. "Okay, no problem. I've got you right here. Just sign this please." She pushed out a piece of paper that we both scrawled our names on. "You can go right through into the conference hall and wait for the welcome address. Everyone else is already here." With a much less friendly 'Hmph!' she picked up the clipboard and walked straight out of the door we'd entered through.

I looked at Fergus. "Was it something you said?"

He shrugged and ran a hand through his dark bouncy hair. "No, I'm sure it's nothing to do with either of us. Let's go through to the conference hall so we can find out what we're in for."

He didn't meet my gaze when he said it. I would have bet the farm that there was something else I wasn't being told by Fergus… and I had no doubt it was another thing that I'd find out later - the hard way.

We walked through into a light and airy magnolia-coloured room. I was surprised to discover how high the ceilings were, but I remembered the strange and sprawling shape and span of the bunker. I knew it would be a difficult place to get to grips with. I looked around and discovered that there was a small group of people standing on the other side of the room, in front of a small raised stage. They all held cups of complimentary coffee in their hands and they were looking at three vases filled with some truly stunning flower arrangements.

"Oh, wow!" I said, forgetting all of my misgivings in the face of these works of art. Were we really going to be learning how to create pieces just like them? I suddenly found I was giddy with excitement. Fergus must have deliberately been toying with me, knowing I wouldn't trust his motivations to come on something as mundane as a flower arranging course. He'd probably wanted to trick me into thinking there was something more going on so that I wouldn't go too mushy on him. I shot him an 'I know the truth' look and then made a beeline for the bouquets. My partner in crime headed for the tea and biscuits.

"...Beautiful colours. Perfect for the coming change of season," an older woman with a very refined voice was saying when I approached the group.

"Those delphiniums are lovely. I wonder what variety they are?" another younger woman asked before looking nervously around, as if seeking approval.

"It's delphinium elatum 'Million Dollar Blue'" I found myself saying automatically. I was so used to people asking questions about the flowers I sold that it slipped right out. I was growing the same variety back home and there was no mistaking its true blue shade and double flowers.

The group turned to look at me with some curiosity. I smiled back, feeling like the new kid in class.

A rotund man with red cheeks and squinting eyes broke the silence that had descended over us all. "It seems to me as though our illustrious guides are running late. Why don't we all get introduced to one another? We're going to be spending the weekend together after all."

There were many murmurs of agreement to this sensible idea.

"I'm Eamon Rushdon, a lecturer on horticulture at Nottingham Trent University," the man who'd suggested the introductions began. He nodded round at everyone in the group in turn, his thin covering of greying hair bobbing with every nod.

"Lady Isabella Duprix." The well-spoken older lady spoke next. Her greying hair was kept neatly under control by shining diamanté pins —or at least, they had to be diamanté, didn't they?— and her outfit looked like it had more in common with the delphinium called 'Million Dollar Blue' than Primark's bargain basement, where I'd been known to source my day-to-day wear. "I'm helping out around the garden on the advice of my doctor in order to keep my mobility ticking over. The gardeners grow so many wonderful flowers, I hope to learn how to create beautiful displays with the proceeds." I could just imagine Lady Duprix showing off her flower arrangements over an afternoon tea with her other wealthy friends. For a brief moment, I felt a stab of envy over the life I perceived her to be leading. Had she worked hard, married for it, or simply been born into the life of luxury? I shook the thoughts from my head. Why was I coveting money? Even if I really did have a million pounds, I would keep on working on my cut flower business. It was everything that made me happy, and it was all I wanted to do - come poverty or riches.

"I'm Duncan and this is my wife, Bella... Smith," a slim man with a few lines already appearing on his face said, hastily adding their last name on the end when he realised that these were formal introductions - as I could only assume was what was acceptable in some of the guests' higher societies. "We won a competition to be here," he confided, looking half-delighted, half-scared sick that there was no way they would fit in with those who'd introduced themselves before. Duncan and Bella looked like a couple you'd expect to see waiting outside of the school gates for their brood to be released. There was certainly nothing outstanding about them, but I knew that courses designed to teach you new skills were a great leveller. Duncan and Bella could display natural talent and an ability to learn that far outstripped even those with prior experience. We would just have to wait and see.

"I'm Tanya Bond. This year, I won a bronze award at Hampton Court Palace Flower Show for my show garden." She shot a sideways look at another woman who stood silently listening before continuing. "However, I think there is a lot of talent and art to arranging flowers. Next year, I hope to enter the professional floristry category. Or perhaps try for a floral exhibit in the marquee." She flicked her annoyingly short fringe off her forehead. It stuck up for a moment before collapsing back. I noticed for the first time that she was wearing a t-shirt branded with her business name: 'Tanya Bond Garden Designs'. For a second, I wondered if I'd missed an opportunity to do the same before I nixed the idea. First of all, I'd never been fond of people who were constantly self-promoting. Secondly, none of us were here to sell ourselves to the other course goers. We were supposed to be here to learn.

"Christine Montague of Montague Royal Designs." The woman Tanya had shot her little sideways look at spoke, introducing herself. Whilst Tanya deflated a little, I took in the woman with the formidable word 'Royal' in her company name. She was tall with raven black hair and a nose that turned up at the end, which gave the impression she was always looking down her nose at anyone who looked back. "This year, I was awarded a Silver-gilt medal at Chelsea Flower Show for my show garden." She frowned. "But it should have been gold." I silently concluded that the nose issue suited her. I wondered if the 'Royal' in her company name was something that could only be added after working for someone from the Royal family itself. I was tempted to ask, but didn't particularly want to encourage the rampant display of egos that seemed to be spiralling upwards towards a crescendo

"Sylvia Rainford. I'm the author of over fifty books on horticulture, botany, floriculture... you name it," an elderly woman said, sipping her tea in a delightfully detached manner that somehow managed to completely dissipate all of the tension that had started to accumulate.

"You're Sylvia Rainford? *The* Sylvia Rainford?" I couldn't help but ask before realising that of course she was. "I loved your book, *The Evolution of Edible Flowers*," I said, knowing I was turning pink.

The old lady smiled. "Edibles can be such fun can't they, dear? I'm glad you enjoyed it."

"I'm Diana Flowers. I own and run a small cut flower business," I said, feeling that it was the right time for me to introduce myself.

"How lovely! British-grown flowers are making a come-back," Sylvia commented, immediately making me feel better for coming across as a fan-girl.

"Rich Strauss at your service." We turned to see a man hanging out next to Fergus by the coffee table. I immediately wondered how I'd failed to notice him when I'd walked into the room. Everything about this guy was, well... noticeable. He was tanned and in excellent shape, either from long hours spent at the gym, or from some kind of manual labour. I reserved my decision as to which it was. Then there was his face. He had the same sideways smile that Fergus did - although, this man's seemed to be a permanent feature, and there was something about his eyes that made you feel like he was looking just at you... and the rest of the room didn't matter one bit.

Uh-oh. I was blushing again.

Then there was the accent.

"I'm here with Christine. I'm her PR guru and a shameless freeloader when it comes to free fancy weekend retreats," he said with his smooth South-African lilt. "You did say that this was a luxury weekend retreat, didn't you?" he asked, drop-ping a wink Christine's way. His stiff-faced employer didn't look amused in the slightest.

"And I'm Fergus Robinson," Fergus said, stepping forwards and opening his arms wide like a circus performer. "Researcher of hidden truths at your service." I half expected him to take a bow after all of the pomp. He

17

was so obviously trying to out-do Rich Strauss's slick intro-duction.

I shot Fergus an amused grin, but the others present seemed genuinely interested.

"Hidden truths?" Eamon enquired.

"I work on proving or disproving theories that have gone unchecked for too long. In doing so, I reveal the truth beneath and enable progress to take place," Fergus said, as vaguely as he could.

"Conspiracy theories?" Tanya had her eyebrows raised up so high they were almost in range of her fringe. I noticed that she shot another sideways glance in Rich's direction... just to see if he was looking her way. Tanya clearly had more on her mind than just flower arranging.

"Well... I wouldn't really call them that..." Fergus blustered.

"Like the theory that this old bunker was the site of an unidentified flying object crash back in the fifties? Are you here to look into that?" She looked genuinely curious. "Hey... I think I've heard of you! I've read your articles." I silently noted that her incredulity had merely been protection until she'd been certain that Fergus was talking about conspiracy theories.

I shot a murderous look in Fergus' direction. I should have trusted my instincts all along! I'd known there was no way he had suddenly developed an interest in flower arrang-ing. He was here because he thought aliens might be taking a stroll nearby.

As soon as the group had lapsed back into quiet chatter I stalked over to the coffee table. "Aliens, Fergus. Really?! I can't believe that I believed you wanted to do this because of some bond of friendship we have!"

"Not necessarily aliens. That was never confirmed. I'm merely interested in any evidence that may suggest an unidentified flying object crash-landed somewhere on this site over sixty years ago."

"You guys argue like an old married couple," Rich jumped in, looking amused by the whole thing.

"We're not a couple," I said at the same time that Fergus said 'We're not married'. We glared at each other.

Rich raised his hands in mock defence. "Whoa now, I never said I needed convincing." He flashed me a white smile, and I felt that stupid blush rise in my cheeks again. This was ridiculous! Had I really stayed away from men for so long that I'd reverted to the awkward behaviorisms of my teenage years? "So, how do you guys know each other?"

Shutters suddenly slammed down into place, covering the windows in the conference room. Bam! The lights shut off. We were thrown into complete darkness.

There were a few sounds of alarm before footsteps could clearly be heard approaching from... somewhere. I felt the air move as someone passed by quite close to me.

A torch flicked on, held beneath someone's chin like a scary storyteller around a campfire. Then, the spectre spoke:

"Ladies and gentlemen... I regret to inform you that this is a life or death situation."

3

SMASHING

A stunned silence fell.

It was then that I realised this whole thing was a set up. If the situation really was life or death, the torch-wielding speaker would not be pausing for dramatic effect.

"The ten of you have three days to get out of here alive. You will be up against challenges tougher than anything any of you has ever faced before. You'll have to work together to overcome impossible odds. You will need to fulfil your potential and perform when the stakes are at their highest. You will have to…" She paused again. "…arrange flowers."

There was a tense couple of seconds, presumably as everyone regained their faculties the way I had. Spontaneous applause broke out. The speaker bowed, her hair flopping forwards over her face. "Thank you, ladies and gentlemen! If you would be so kind as to follow me through the doorway at the back of the stage, you will enter the main bunker and I will trigger the lockdown. No one can get in or out for the next fifty-two hours. If you complete your tasks and conquer the challenges, the door will open at the end of day three. If you fail, or do not finish in time..."

BANG!

The beam of the torch swung round and illuminated the central flower arrangement. The vase had broken in two, shattered by some unseen force. *Most likely a hidden mechanism,* I concluded. Even though I knew how it was done, it didn't make it any less ominous.

"She's kidding, right? Nothing bad will actually happen, will it?" I whispered in Fergus' ear.

I was close enough to feel him shrug his shoulders. "Did you read the waiver form we signed on the way in? It will all have been written in there, so you can't sue the organisers afterwards. You probably should have read it you know."

"What the heck did it say?!" I hissed, not finding his words comforting.

"I don't know. I didn't read it."

Up on the stage the speaker produced another torch with a wider beam that lit the room a little better. "My name is Lorna. I will be one of your guides on this first-of-its-kind course. Please leave all electronic devices in the box in front of the door. If you try to keep any, the buzzer will sound when you pass through the door, and you will not be permitted to proceed. Watch your step!" she said, flashing the light down to the floor when we all walked through the doorway at the back of the stage. It was the first time she'd really broken character and said something, well... normal! For just a second, I was reassured that this wasn't as nutty as I'd feared.

"This course is fully interactive. You will be learning from some of the best in the industry as you proceed through the challenges. Listen well and perform the tasks to the highest standards and you will move on to the next challenge. Your mentors have also set the gradings of your final work. The latest technology allows a computer to evaluate your creations and make a decision as to whether or not you've passed or failed." Lorna stopped walking. "Remember - failure can be fatal. This is a high risk, high reward education experience - as per the waivers you all signed on the way in."

"It would have been nice if someone had told me that that was what it was..." I heard Eamon grumble. For a moment, I was pleased that I wasn't the only one who'd missed that vital piece of information.

"That lovely receptionist did tell you. I heard her very clearly. You were too busy trying to flirt, you old wind bag!" I heard a clipped voice reply. I thought that it probably belonged to Christine. I remembered my own encounter with the receptionist and the way she'd reacted to Fergus and then changed her tune before leaving the bunker. I was willing to bet that she'd forgotten, deliberately or otherwise, to inform us of that crucial detail she'd surely been employed to pass on.

"Did anyone read it before they signed?" Rich's South African accent cut through the darkness. He sounded perpetually amused.

No one spoke up.

Fantastic. I was stuck on a course being described as 'life or death' with a group of people who didn't read the fine print. I knew that I was included in that category, but it was hardly fair...

"Here we go!" Lorna announced once we were all standing in the dark room behind the stage, having forsaken our gadgets. With a dramatic flourish she pulled down a lever. A loud alarm sounded and the door we'd come through slid back onto place and a giant counter displaying fifty-two hours started counting down. Our guide grinned. "Time's a ticking! We'd better get to our first challenge."

As soon as she said it, the lights snapped on in the room. There was a man standing waiting by a row of tables.

"Welcome everyone. My name is Jack, and along with Lorna, we will be your guides on this first ever course of its kind. As my colleague just said, time is already running out. We must begin our first challenge, so if you can all find a work station, everything will be explained…"

We all shuffled into place. I noticed that the atmosphere was a lot more tense than it had been when we'd been introducing ourselves. However, I also felt that the egos had left the room. Everyone had been shaken up by the shocking start - which must not have explicitly been advertised when they'd signed up for the course. Now it felt like we were on a level playing field.

A screen that covered the entire wall in front of us snapped on.

"Hello? Can you all hear me?" a smiling older lady said, seeming to peer through the camera at us. "Hello?"

"Hello! We can hear you," Jack said, before turning to face us. "All of these videos have been prerecorded by our teachers, however, the latest technology has allowed us to make them fully interactive. If you have a question, just ask and you will receive a response.

"Oh, good! I just wanted to check this was working," the kindly-looking lady on screen continued. "Welcome to the Fennering Bunker. I'm Emilia Payne - author and award-winning florist. As you are aware, you will be learning the intricacies of arranging flowers, and much more besides, over the next few days. Now, as your lovely guides have already mentioned, time is already running out, so I'm going to get straight on to your first challenge. We are going to begin with the basics. In front of you now there will be a vase and a pre-cut bouquet…" There was a mechanical whirring and everyone's workspace opened up to reveal a vase and a posy, just as Emilia had described. "You will notice that all of the vases and flowers are different from one another. You will be placing these pre-cut flowers in the vase correct for their height. Bouquets should be about one and a half times the height of the container they are in. However, when you find there may be more than one option available to you, you may also want to consider the size of your container's opening and the type of bouquet you are trying to display." Her eyes twinkled. "You will soon discover that, whilst you will be honing your individual skills, the group will advance as a team, and this particular exercise must be completed as a team. Work together, make the correct choices, and you will advance to the next challenge."

Emilia stopped speaking and stood, seeming to watch patiently with her hands clasped in front of her.

"Hey, what if we need the loo?" Rich asked, grinning and cocking an eyebrow around. "Just saying! I hope the smart guys who designed this course have thought of that little detail."

Emilia smiled. "That is an excellent question. Washroom facilities will always be accessible. They are either located in the challenge rooms through a separate door, or close by on a route that will open for you, should you wish to use the facilities."

"Well... thank goodness for that!" Rich said, still grinning.

I looked down at the stubby bouquet of mauve flowers and the long and slender vase I'd been left with. They certainly weren't the correct partners. I reached out and picked up the bouquet. I didn't recognise the flowers themselves, but I was already all-too aware that there were still gaping holes in my floriculture knowledge. They were short and had thick stems but fairly large heads. I was looking for a stout container, and not a large one. I cast my eyes around the room and saw a beaten copper cauldron sitting in front of Rich Strauss. With great trepidation I walked over and plonked in the bouquet.

"Looks good to me," he said, flashing me a white grin. "Where do you think these go?" he asked, showing me a fat bunch of eucalyptus and greenery, with some autumnal blackberries and rose hips giving a splash of colour.

We looked around together and discovered others were doing the same. I could already see one other bouquet had been placed and primped by Tanya. She looked up and smiled at Rich, flashing her teeth.

Not everyone was doing so well.

Christine was trying to place her long-stemmed larkspur into a tall vase whilst Eamon shook a fistful of amaryllis in her face. It was clear that they had reached an impasse - just as Emilia had predicted. I spied another tall vase, but with a wider opening, in front of a bewildered-looking Duncan.

"How about this?" I said, entering the fray with the new vase. "Amaryllises have thick stems. They would cope better with a wider-topped vase. Larkspurs could just flop everywhere." I knew that much from hard-learned experience.

Eamon considered the new vessel I held in my hands. "Yes, well, I suppose you could be right," he said and tentatively placed the amaryllis flowers in the vase.

"They look good," I said, shooting him a smile.

Christine triumphantly primped her larkspur arrangement, a smug smile on her face for all to see. "Tut, tut! You should always know when to listen to your superiors. I have a degree in structural engineering. I could match flowers to vases in my sleep."

I bit my lip to keep from commenting and happened to meet the eyes of a startled looking Rich. We'd been told that this entire course was built on teamwork, but it would appear that some people didn't play nicely with others - even during the first challenge.

For the most part, we all helped one another. The only real struggle we had at the end was when we discovered we had one more vase than we had bouquets. That led to some heated discussion as to whether several of our choices were actually correct. Our dilemma was solved when Fergus dropped the vase that the majority had hated, but a minority were arguing was perfect for an equally ugly flower-arrangement.

"Whoops!" he said, dropping me a wink when no one else was looking. I shut my eyes and prayed that this interactive course had taken someone like Fergus into account. Otherwise, that broken vase could mean we were stuck in this tiny room for the next fifty-two hours. That would be plenty of time to tell Fergus exactly what I felt about this entire mess he'd dragged me into... and all because he'd wanted to look for little green men!

With a complete lack of aplomb, Fergus dumped the ugly bouquet into the remaining container.

We all turned back to Emilia to learn our fate, having displayed the vases and bouquets on the front table. She narrowed her eyes and seemed to take them in.

"Well, well! You've all been listening. All of these bouquets are correctly placed. You will have noticed that there was a surplus container. It was included as a red herring. You quite rightly observed that it held no water inside it - thus making it not suitable to hold a bouquet at all! It is an ancient milk jug that was dug up on the land Fennering Bunker was built on. The course organisers and I thought it would be a nice idea to include some of our ancient history to add a little zest to this challenge." Her eyes looked fondly at the table where, presumably, her pre-recorded form believed there would be a milk jug amongst the line-up.

Everyone turned to look at Fergus.

He cleared his throat. "Ah, yes... come to think of it, there *was* no water inside. I forgot flowers like water. On the plus side, at least it's just shards to clear up. No messy water…"

I shut my eyes for a moment even while the door opened to lead us through to the next room and the next challenge. The course organisers had designed everything with both beginners and experts in mind. However, they hadn't accounted for Fergus. I wondered if he would end up being our undoing or our salvation.

Fortunately, the next two challenges were fairly idiot-proof. There were no similar reprises of the milk jug incident and everyone was in a fairly confident mood when we were released from the maze of rooms. We were informed the area we'd arrived in was the dinner hall and also the site of our rooms. We were allowed fifteen minutes to settle in, freshen up, and take our luggage from the main hall to our rooms before the bell rang to inform us that lunch was ready to be served.

"Welcome to your third challenge," a voice announced. We all turned to discover a screen sliding down across the hall from us. The top of the table in front of the screen smoothly lifted off to reveal a row of sandwiches, cakes, and pastries. A man in a chef's hat smiled around at us all.

"So far, you've had it easy…" he began, even as Fergus walked up to the table to inspect the offerings.

"You're right about that!" Christine sniped, examining her manicured nails with a smirk on her face. Next to her, Bella and Duncan looked crestfallen. I noticed Lady Isabella shot the prestigious designer a scathing look, but being a well-bred lady, she didn't stoop to pass comment.

"…but now the stakes are much higher. In front of you, is a delicious spread of food for your lunch. All of these culinary creations are botanically inspired. You will find flowers and plants have been used in each. In front of the dishes on display is a small sample of the plants or flowers used in each of the dishes. Only…" he paused for dramatic effect. "…one of them is poisonous."

There was the sound of someone loudly choking. Fergus turned around from the table, his mouth full of fairy cake.

4

FLYING SAUCERS

"Has he been poisoned?" Sylvia whispered, sounding freakishly intrigued by the prospect. There was some truth to what they said about some old ladies having a fascination with all things morbid.

I strolled over to the table and glanced at the flower sample on the plate in front of the cakes Fergus had got stuck into without waiting.

"What's the prognosis, Doc? Am I going to die?" he asked.

It was the sideways smile that made me do it.

"Bad news. It's deadly nightshade."

Fergus' eyes widened. His smile vanished. "I'm going to die, aren't I?" he whispered.

"They're violet flowers. You're fine. But I hope you learned your lesson," I told him, feeling like the long-suffering parent of a very badly behaved child.

Fergus looked at the half-eaten fairy cake in his hand. After a second of further thought, he popped it into his mouth and took another. "Dig in everyone! This pile is good to go."

The man on the screen continued as if nothing exceedingly idiotic had happened. "The poison in question is not deadly, however, it will certainly give you a bad stomach, so keep your eyes peeled! I'm sure some of you will be thinking: 'But this is flower arranging! Why would I need to know about poisonous plants?' and I am going to give you an answer to that question. When we create flower arrangements, we must always keep our clients in mind. While no one would expect a client to eat an entire bouquet - unless that's your selling point - it is important to know if you are including any truly harmful plants in order to inform clients and any who might be affected." He smiled. "Now... one of you has some experience of edible and poisonous plants, so I will be leaving you in her capable hands. I hope that she will share her knowledge with all of you. I mentioned that this is higher stakes, and as you already know, this course favours team work. In this particular challenge, you will be relying on the strengths of one of you to keep you all safe. There will be no check and correct at the end of this, so identify and eat with care. Good luck!"

I glared at Fergus who was still stuffing cakes into his mouth.

"What?! I'm hungry! There weren't any good biscuits with the coffee and it was ages ago. I'd have packed a lunch if I'd known there was a risk of being poisoned," he protested.

I turned to look at Sylvia, the author of The Evolution of Edible Flowers and the woman the man on screen had surely been referring to. She walked over to the table and then beckoned me.

"Just between us, dear, my eyesight is not what is used to be! I know I wrote *Poisonous Plants of the British Isles,* but I can't actually see half of these little flowers and leaves. Do you think that you might be able to pick the bad one from the bunch? You know about edible flowers, don't you?" Sylvia whispered to me.

I looked at the row of flowers and food in front of us. I'd already spotted the violets, Dahlia petals, and mint leaves, but there were a few others I had questions about. The first was a plate of innocuous-looking red berries. I walked over and picked one up. It wasn't a redcurrant, that was for sure, but it could still be edible. As I child, I'd been taught not to eat red berries, but I knew it was just a safety precaution. Not all wild red berries were poisonous and it was often berries that were darker or lighter colours that were far more risky.

"Look at the leaves," Sylvia said, following me closely.

"I'm not that good at berry identification," I muttered. I was a floriculturist, and not an experienced one at that. But, as I looked closely, I thought I did recognise the plant the berry had originated from by its distinctive leaf. "Is it rowan?" I asked a little tentatively.

Sylvia nodded. "I think so. They are naughty to slip this one in. It's a real red herring. They won't have just used the berries as they are, I'm sure it's rowan berry jam in those sponge cakes."

I looked despondently along the row of plates with their questionable samples. Whoever had designed this little challenge had relied upon Sylvia being the one to do this. Were we all going to end up poisoned because of me? I reassured myself that we'd been told it wouldn't be fatal. But that didn't mean the others wouldn't kill me if I got this wrong...

Hang on. What was that innocuous looking green and yellow plant? I walked over and looked at the slim green leaves and green-yellow blooms that weren't exactly un-leaf-like in their appearance either. "That's a spurge," I muttered, thinking out loud for the most part.

"Euphorbia?" Sylvia said, overhearing me. "Oh, those rotters! That's some nasty stuff. I supposed on the plus side, it's reputed to taste so bitter that one wouldn't persist in eating it for long. Baked into shortbread or otherwise." She inclined her head towards the plate of biscuits that I knew I certainly wouldn't be touching.

"Don't be so sure about that." I was thinking of Fergus when I said it. In one decided movement, I picked up the plate of biscuits and dumped them in the bin. "Was spurge in your poisonous plants book?" I asked Sylvia. Her book on edible flowers had merely carried a few precautions about lookalike varieties that could be mistaken for edibles and then a few varieties of flowers within edible flower families that couldn't, or shouldn't, actually be eaten. I knew about sun spurge in particular because it insisted on growing on my land. I'd toyed with the idea of incorporating it into bouquets before learning even the sap was an irritant.

"It was in the poison plant book I wrote," she confirmed. "I meant it as a sort of diagnostic manual for parents with children who have curious fingers and mouths, however, I don't think that's the only market who bought it. It was really rather successful," the elderly lady said, looking a little troubled.

I silently wondered if there was a correlation between her book's release and any rise in poisonings in the country. I decided I probably didn't want to find out.

We stuck with the basics of floristry during the afternoon, but even the basics were hard to master. Those who'd walked in with large egos and extensive previous experience were forced to assist others or watch the group sink. And even they didn't always get it right. I was especially smug when Christine's snapdragon and sea lavender arrangement was criticised for being fuddy-duddy. Whomever had designed this course had obviously been expecting some of the attendees to have some pretty old-fashioned flower arranging ideas. She was told to mix things up a bit and resubmit by the virtual teacher. When that didn't fly with Christine, Bella stepped in and jazzed the arrangement up a little by adding some curling ivy and eucalyptus accents. This was praised and the group moved on.

In spite of the grumbles of a few of the group when their work was criticised, all of our actions seemed to have been accounted for... with the notable exception of Fergus. I'd never seen a virtual recording falter so many times than when faced with Fergus' questions and everything he produced. In the end, I'd taken to finishing my own task and then forcing whatever he was working on into submission.

"But I like what I'm doing!" Fergus said when I stopped him from trying to combine bright red chrysanthemums with yellow and pink snapdragons. It wouldn't have been so bad if this challenge hadn't been focusing on tasteful colour combinations. A single stalk of eucalyptus and a green spiky fern had also been added haphazardly to the vase.

"It's either a fabulous work of modern art or a complete disaster," I told him, knowing which one I was leaning towards. "You don't want to learn flower arranging. You're not even giving it a chance! You're just here to find evidence of aliens."

"That's not true!" Fergus protested. "I'm also here for the food. It's supposedly been created by a top chef. Poisoning aside, it has been pretty good."

I rolled my eyes. "You could at least pretend to be trying."

"I am trying! This beautiful bouquet is exactly what's needed to shake the floral world up a bit. Just watch..." Before I could stop him, he marched over to the display podium and plonked his vase down to be judged.

The kindly lady looked down at it for a moment as the arrangement was judged virtually.

RUBY LOREN

"See! She's going to love it!" Fergus whispered right before an alarm sounded.

Everyone jumped and looked up, trying to find the source of the noise.

All of a sudden, the top of the display table flipped up, catapulting Fergus' arrangement against the wall. The vase smashed and the flowers gracefully slid down to the floor, some clinging on to the wallpaper.

I raised my eyebrows. "Someone did see you coming after all."

On screen the kindly lady smiled. "We know when you're not paying attention. At this stage in the course, you all understand how high the stakes are. Those who deliberately ignore our teachings will find out the consequences the hard way."

"That's not ominous at all," Fergus said, looking at what remained of his arrangement.

I seized a bunch of eucalyptus and some sensible soft blues and pale pink coloured flowers, slapping the lot down on the table in front of him. "Time to start taking something seriously... for once." I shot him a smug smile.

Fergus scowled, crossing his arms and looking thoroughly put out by the humiliation he'd just been subjected to. "If I'd known I was actually going to have to learn something on this course, I'd never have signed up for it! Learning should be optional."

I thought Fergus had been practicing that principle for quite some time. Somehow, I managed to keep my mouth shut.

The final challenge before dinner and the end of our first day was a big finish. Much like some popular TV shows, we were instructed to produce a showstopper that put into practice everything we'd learnt today. A time limit had been set for the challenge, and everyone had to pass or we would all be stuck without dinner until everyone made the grade. I was working on combining delphiniums and hydrangeas in a bold but beautiful bunch, when Rich came over to talk to me.

"Looks good!" he commented, before toying with a stalk of sea lavender. "So... you grow flowers, right? As a business?"

I inclined my head. "You said you work in PR?" I was half-wondering if I was about to be pitched in some way. If Rich thought I was some kind of big deal in the floral industry, he was sorely mistaken.

He shrugged self-deprecatingly. "I know how to talk a good game, and people pay me well for it. That's all it really is. I grew up near Cape Town. You'll have to trust me when I say that you need to be able to talk yourself out of trouble when you live there. It was easy to carry it over to my work."

"Was it a rough neighbourhood?" I didn't have much idea about what life was like in South Africa. It was strange to me that everything about the man I was talking to seemed so familiar - so British, even. And yet, he'd grown up half the world away.

He shrugged. "I'm sure it was no different from any big city really. Not back then anyway. I just used to go looking for trouble. I was the kind of kid who'd run off to go rock climbing in the wilderness without any safety devices, or see how close I could get to poking a puff adder." He grinned at the memories of his reckless youth. "Hey, what's the deal with the guy you came with? I'm no flower expert, but he seems to know less than the couple who won their way here."

I was pleased that Duncan and Bella were out of earshot when he said the last part. "I think that everyone has some-thing to offer - no matter their previous level of experience."

Rich raised his tanned hands in defence. "I didn't mean to upset you or be harsh to anyone else. I thought I was just stating the facts. Bella and Duncan are doing great. They're knocking the socks off what I can do. But Fergus…" We both looked across to where the man himself was arranging snap-dragons and trailing ivy with great exuberance but not a lot of actual skill - or regard for anything we'd learned today. "… it's like he's not even trying. Why is he here if he doesn't want to learn floristry? It's not his job right? Or anything like that?"

I opened my mouth and shut it again, feeling guilty. "He did book this course as a birthday present to me," I confessed, wondering again if I had harshly judged his motives for coming here. I knew from past experience that Fergus had no qualms about sniffing around on someone else's land. If he'd wanted to come looking for aliens, surely he'd have done it a long time ago? Technical things like 'having permission to be on someone else's property' didn't tend to slow Fergus down.

Rich's eyebrows shot up. "Oh, so you're together then?"

"No, we aren't," I said, immediately realising what he was getting at. At that precise moment Fergus turned around and flashed me a grin and two thumbs up. I shook my head at him and his hideous arrangement. I would go and talk to him about fixing it, just as soon as my conversation with Rich was done. For just a second, I thought his smile faltered before he turned back to his failing flower arrangement.

"Interesting," Rich said, looking me straight in the eye with his intense hazel gaze.

I cleared my throat and stabbed a delphinium cone into my arrangement at random. Emilia had advised us all that random flair could sometimes pay dividends… "You should probably be getting back to your showstopper. It looks nice," I told him, inclining my head towards his pink, white, and violet display. It looked like it was close to completion.

"Sure, you're probably right. Oh, you can't be serious!" he said, his tone of voice suddenly changing. I followed his gaze past me and realised that Christine had just gone over to talk to Fergus. Rich turned back to me with his eyebrows raised again. "I never thought I'd see the day when my boss would help someone other than herself. I know everyone talks about their bosses being dragons, but she's as inhuman and scaly as they come. I guess that's what it takes to be a success in this biz." He grinned, lightening the moment. "That and a fabulous PR guy, of course." With a final wink, he returned to his work station. I pretended not to notice the curious looks directed my way from the florists close by to me when he walked away again.

"You'll want to be careful with that young man. I've been courted by my fair share. I know that type when I see it. They never stay around for long," Lady Isabella said from her position on the work bench next to me.

I looked at her in amazement, but she was already back to focusing on her hydrangeas as if she'd never said a word.

***

With Christine's astonishing intervention, we passed the final challenge of the day. There was an air of relief when we were released from the fresh maze of rooms and returned down winding corridors to the dinner hall.

"How did you find the final challenge?" I asked Fergus once we were out of earshot of the group. I already had strong suspicions that everyone wanted to nose into everyone else's business. After all - what else did we have to entertain ourselves with no electronic devices allowed? I hoped everyone had packed a few paperbacks.

"It was great. Christine said I had a real flair for design. I think she might take me on as a protege in her company when we finish up here," Fergus said with such seriousness that I stared at him agog.

"You're joking."

"I am," he confirmed with an eye roll of his own. I supposed it was probably payback. "If you must know, she wanted to talk about a business matter."

"What kind of business matter?" I couldn't possibly imagine what the pair may have in common.

Fergus was acting all superior and lofty. "If you must know... she's heard of me and has read a couple of the articles I've written in the past. She wanted to employ my services."

I waited for further explanation. What could Christine Montague possibly want with a conspiracy theorist like Fergus? "Well...?" I prompted when he stayed silent.

"I couldn't possibly comment on a confidential..."

"Fergus!" I interrupted, peeved he was going to try that with me.

"All right. I'll tell you what she wanted if you tell me what you were talking about with that slime bag, Rich."

"Slime bag? Do I detect a hint of jealousy?" I joked, amused that Fergus had even been paying that much attention.

"No jealousy here. Just a knowledge of the male brain."

"I don't know whether I should be flattered or offended." I said before sighing. "Rich asked me about my flower business and then said he didn't think you wanted to learn anything about flower arranging. He was wondering why you came on the course. I told him it was because of my birthday. I didn't tell him the actual truth."

Fergus tried to act innocent.

"If we get stuck here or something bad happens to us because of you sneaking around looking for flying saucers, I'm going to kill you," I told him. I frowned. "How did you get us on this course anyway? From everything I've seen only industry influencers and the very wealthy were allowed in -

with the exception of competition winners. Neither of us are big names in the flower industry. Or wealthy," I added, looking sideways at Fergus in case he wished to contradict me.

He threw me a knowing glance but stayed silent on that matter. He still wasn't going to tell me how he made his living. "I told you - I have contacts. If you must know, Jack and I go way back," he said, talking about the male guide. "The course was full until the guy that was supposed to be here instead of us suddenly got ill. I pulled some strings and Jack got us in last minute. Pretty thoughtful of me, eh?"

"It might have been, had you not said that last part," I sniped.

Fergus nodded as though I hadn't reprimanded him at all. "It's the first time Fennering Bunker has been opened up to anyone since its esteemed owner Sir Gordon Laird locked the place up tight. That was after all of the reports about what happened here in the fifties came to light a couple of decades after it had all gone down. It was only then that the military finally moved out. No one, not even a conspiracy theorist with contacts, has been able to get a sniff of this bunker... until now." His eyes sparkled with mischief. "The rest of The Truth Beneath are going to be green with envy when they find out where I've spent the weekend."

"You **are** only here for that!" I couldn't believe I'd been persuading myself to think of Fergus' motivations more favourably. "I defended you!" I said, thinking of my conversation with Rich.

"You needn't have done. I'm used to cynics and those who disagree with my methods. It will all be worth it in the end."

I threw my head back and made a sound of disgust. "Oh, please... don't act the martyr with me. I know exactly how you like to play your games," I told him, determined to stalk off and enjoy some dinner without Fergus' annoying presence. With a bit of luck, it wouldn't be poisoned this time.

"Didn't you want to know what Christine spoke to me about?"

I hesitated mid-stalk, ruining my dramatic exit. "Fine," I confessed, my curiosity getting the better of me. See? I should have packed a paperback. Then I'd never have cared so much about idle gossip.

"She's actually pretty paranoid. Christine believes that someone on this course might be out to get her because of some shady business past of hers." He waved a hand to show it was inconsequential. "She reckons she's got a lot of enemies."

"Shocking," I said, thinking of the rather low opinion I'd formed of the garden designer in less than a day spent with her.

"I asked her if she knew anyone on the course, other than Rich. She said she didn't, and she trusts her PR guy. Beyond that, she wouldn't say why she thought someone was going to do something to her." Fergus shrugged. "I told her that I'm not a detective, and that there is nothing I can do if she isn't going to share the whole truth with me. I know she's holding something back, but I've no idea what it could be. When she didn't want to say anything more we left it. That was it."

I frowned. "Do you really think she's in some kind of trouble." I shot Fergus a sideways look under my eyelids, just to check his reaction.

A slow sideways smile appeared on his face. "Who's the jealous one now?"

Apparently, I hadn't been that subtle.

The smell of roast duck wafted down the corridor, and I felt my mouth beginning to water. We walked into the dining hall to find everyone looking at the platter of duck breast and dauphinoise potatoes with suspicion.

"Don't mind me," Fergus said... skipping to the front of the queue and piling up a plate. Everyone watched as he speared a forkful of duck and potatoes and stuck it into his mouth, chewing thoughtfully. "Delicious!"

I silently thought that this course might need someone like Fergus after all - someone reckless enough to dive straight into dinner after nearly being poisoned at lunch. There was one thing about Fergus that I couldn't deny - his spirit seemed to be utterly unquenchable.

It didn't escape my notice that everyone else waited for a whole minute to pass before they actually started eating.

"What are you doing?" I asked when Fergus followed me to my room carrying his suitcase.

"Coming to bed."

"Excuse me?"

Fergus slapped his forehead like something had just slipped his mind. I folded my arms. "Did I forget to say earlier? We got in because someone was sick. There was one room for him... but obviously I asked for two tickets." He turned his palms up as if to say 'what could I do?'

Fergus pushed the door open. "Mmm looks cosy!" He plumped down on the bed to the right of the room. When he saw my face he grinned. "Look on the bright side... at least it's two twins and not a double."

I threw a pillow at him. "You'd better not get any ideas."

Fergus stretched out on his bed. "The only idea I have is to get some sleep. Didn't you hear? Tomorrow is going to be an even tougher day. I won't make star florist if I don't get some shut-eye."

If there'd been another pillow to throw, it would have followed the first.

"May I have my pillow back?" I asked, feeling annoyance itching at my fingertips. This was just so typical of Fergus.

My unwanted roommate considered the pillow he'd held onto after it had made contact with his face. "No," he decided before rolling over and covering himself up with a blanket.

"Fergus…" I threatened, but it would appear my rash act of pillow-violence was being punished.

"Goodnight, Diana. Don't forget that tomorrow is your birthday! I think it's going to be one for the history books."

I lay down on my own bed without bothering to take off the clothes I'd been wearing that day. I wasn't going to change in front of Fergus anyway.

I considered how much I wanted to murder Fergus for dragging me on this insane course as a cover for him, so he could snoop around after extraterrestrials. Was it enough to offer him a spurge shortbread? I reserved that decision for the following day.

I woke up to a loud bang.

The room was dark and I could hear Fergus snoring in the blackness. My first feeling was annoyance. It had taken me forever to get to sleep with all of the noise coming from my roommate's sinuses. The next moment, I was completely alert. The course guides had claimed that the challenges would commence again tomorrow morning. A glance at the glow in the dark alarm clock on the bedside table informed me that it was 2:10 a.m. - which was technically morning. Could this be another twist in this unusual flower arranging course, or was someone in trouble?

With great trepidation, I stuck my head out of the door and looked up and down the corridor. Lorna was walking down the row of doors with a flashlight in her hand.

"Did you make a noise?" she asked me.

I shook my head. "I think it came from the right," I said, indicating the direction that I believed the bang had come from. "There hasn't been any sound since."

"Is everything all right?" Lorna gently called in the general direction. When there was no answer, she reached out and jiggled a door handle before shrugging. It was locked.

"Yes, fine. I just saw a spider and broke a mug," a female voice said from behind the locked door.

"Okay, sleep tight!" Lorna answered before shrugging in my direction.

"Night," I said to the guide, returning to my room. I shut the door behind me and sat on my bed, listening to the sounds of Fergus snoring. As I lay back, it occurred to me that it was officially my birthday. I was 29-years-old. All thoughts of everything that had changed and all that I'd achieved over the past year swam through my head. All things considered, it had been a good one - the best I'd ever known. My business had blossomed, and I got to work at something I was passionate about. What did I really have to complain about? As long as things continued on this trajectory, all would be well. I was happy. I smiled in the darkness, finally able to see that, while my birthday itself may not be without turbulence, I had a lot to be thankful for.

I shut my eyes and managed to drift off to sleep again.

The next time I woke up, it was 3:30 a.m. I thought that a series of muffled thumps had drawn me back to consciousness. Next, in the dead silence that followed, someone screamed. The door being slammed shocked me fully awake. I sprung out of bed and flung open the door, only pausing for a millisecond to shoot a disbelieving look in Fergus' direction. How was he sleeping through this mayhem?

I looked up and down the corridor and saw someone

running away. It was a man wearing some kind of military uniform... and glowing with a sort of greenish light. I blinked but the apparition didn't change. I wasn't dreaming.

"Hey!" I called, wondering who (or what) they were, and what they were doing here. My mind immediately jumped to Fergus' claims that this bunker had been used to conceal evidence of an extraterrestrial's crash landing. Wouldn't a strange glowing figure fit with that theory? "What am I thinking?" I muttered before jogging after the disappearing figure. The lack of sleep was definitely getting to me if I was starting to entertain ridiculous rumours.

"Is everything all right?" Jack approached from the opposite direction to the way the apparition had fled.

A door was thrown open. Sylvia Rainford stumbled out dressed in a white nightgown. "Someone was in my room. There was a man! He was in my room!"

"Ma'am, there can't have been anyone in your room... unless it was one of the other guests. Did you lock your door?" Jack asked, not looking convinced by her account.

"Of course I locked my door!" Sylvia said, her shock giving way to anger. "He didn't get in **that** way, I'm sure of it. I left my window open. It's stuffy. I woke up and he was in my room standing over my bed!"

I walked over to her open door and looked through. Sure enough, the window was wide open. As to whether anyone had passed through it, I couldn't say. The rooms were on the ground floor of the bunker, but I'd already looked out of my own window and had estimated that we were a couple of metres off the ground. It wasn't inconceivable that someone had climbed in, but I'd have thought they'd probably have needed a ladder.

"What happened next?" Jack asked, not doing a very good job of sounding convinced.

"When I saw him, I screamed. He ran to my door and

unlocked it from the inside, where I'd left the key in the door. Then he was gone," Sylvia explained.

"I saw someone running down the corridor," I confessed.

"There! You see? She believes me," Sylvia said, shooting me a warm look whilst freezing Jack out.

"Where did this person go?" our guide queried, now looking disdainfully at me - as if it were my fault for seeing something that actually corroborated Sylvia's story.

"Down that way," I said, pointing. "Does it go anywhere that an intruder might want to break into?"

"It's a dead end. There's a door, but it's locked. I think it leads to an area of the bunker that hasn't been included in this course. A lot of this old building still needs renovation done after years of neglect. We get to see the nice parts, but there are areas that are very much the original bunker, and they look exactly as you'd expect."

I nodded, toying with the idea of walking down after whomever it was that had gone that way. Either they would be waiting in front of that dead end door in the darkness, or they must have slipped into one of the rooms at the side when I'd been distracted by Jack's arrival and Sylvia's dramatic turn. That was - if it truly was a dead end.

"Did you see who it was?" Jack asked.

"They were wearing a military uniform I think. It was dark," I confessed, not entirely sure of what I'd seen myself. I cleared my throat, summoning my courage for the last part. "Also... they were glowing with a greenish light. I'm sure there's a logical explanation." I wanted to make that much clear. I was not claiming anything outlandish or paranormal had occurred.

Jack was looking more cheesed off by the second. "Right. I don't think there's anyone around here now. We should try and get some more sleep."

"I won't be sleeping a wink after that. It's outrageous! I

thought the whole point of this course was for it to be at a secure location. You can't have people coming in here as they please." Sylvia spun on her heel and flounced back into her room. There was a final click as she locked the door behind her.

Jack looked at me in the darkness. "Do you actually think there was someone in her room?" he asked, keeping his voice low.

"I really did see that man running down the corridor," I repeated.

Jack looked a little more unsettled. "Maybe it was someone playing a joke - one of the guests I mean. There really is good security in this place. No one is getting in or out. No one's ever managed to break-into Fennering Bunker - even after it was retired as a military base. I know a lot of people have tried." I silently thought of Fergus and knew that Jack was probably alluding to him and other groups and individuals like him. Fergus had told me that he and Jack had some kind of shared history. "I bet she didn't really remember to lock the door. Or maybe someone did manage to shimmy out of their own window and through hers for a joke. I can't think who'd have the strength for it. Or the will!" He shook his head. "It's funny. I thought a group of flower arrangers would be a quiet lot."

"How do you know Fergus?" I asked, changing the subject.

"We go way back," he said, echoing Fergus' own words. "He used to come round and go metal-detecting with my old man. He was like an uncle to me growing up. When I was a teenager, he took me with him when he broke into this aban-doned observatory. It was super cool to have an adult around who was nuts enough to do something like that."

I shut my eyes for a moment. Trust Fergus to be helping

teenagers to break the law rather than encouraging them to keep it!

"He's a great guy," Jack finished, sensing my unspoken opinion.

"I know that," I told him, resignation in my voice. I really did. For all of Fergus' peculiar beliefs and erratic behaviour, I knew that his core was good. He was honourable and he was loyal. He was also a pain in the ass, but deep down, I believed that I would always see him as one of my greatest friends. *Possibly even my best friend!* I suddenly realised, mentally watching my old friends becoming more distant and Fergus sticking with me. I still wasn't quite sure how we'd fitted together, but we had. As crazy as it might sound, I was glad.

"Good night, Jack," I said to the sleepy guide. He lifted a hand in farewell and then walked back down the corridor in the opposite direction to where I'd seen the strange figure run. For the briefest of moments, at that early hour, I considered the possibility of a paranormal explanation. This was an old military bunker. Might both Sylvia and I have seen a remnant of the bunker's military past, wandering the corridors and vanishing without a trace? I was certainly glad that no one - especially Fergus - was there to witness my moment of doubt. Ghosts were implausible and there was zero concrete proof for their existence. In all of history, no one had managed to provide any evidence to support the physical manifestation of a single phantom. While I was always willing to keep an open mind when it came to science, I thought that the odds were heavily stacked against Casper the ghost.

Someone had been messing around. Perhaps it had even been Jack himself, trying to scare guests. He could have lied about the corridor being a dead end, and he must know the bunker better than we visitors. He might have gone through the window and... I shook my head, deciding I wasn't going to stay up all night dwelling on it.

I returned to my room, made a sound of despair when I saw the time on the clock, and then slept undisturbed until the morning - when I woke up to the sound of a loud bang and someone screaming.

5

ONE OF US

I blinked at the daylight coming in through the curtains. Fergus was still snoring.

"Fergus, wake up! There was a bang and then someone screamed," I hissed, deciding that I wasn't going to face this fresh incident alone.

"Mmmm what's happening?" He rolled over and looked at me with clear eyes. "Why'd you wake me up? I was sleeping!"

"Someone screamed," I repeated, not feeling too charitable towards the man across the room from me. As far as I could tell, he'd slept like a baby. Unlike me.

Fergus rolled over. "Maybe someone popped their clogs. A few of our neighbours did look as though they were buddying up with the grim reaper, if you know what I mean."

"Fergus!" I said, horrified that he would joke about something like that.

"Death shouldn't be such a faux pas," he replied, sitting up and looking at me for the first time. "You look terrible. Is this the truth beneath the make up? I feel like I've been deceived."

"Hey! You're not a picture yourself, Sleeping Beauty. I just didn't sleep well. Unlike some," I couldn't help adding.

Fergus frowned. "I thought the beds were pretty comfy. Why didn't you sleep?"

"I'll write you a list," I said drily. I walked to the door and opened it. There was a small gathering in the corridor outside. Lorna was being comforted by Tanya and Bella. Eamon was looking into the open door of one of the rooms with a grim expression on his face.

"What's happened?" I asked, noting the looks of distress.

"I don't think you should come any closer. It's not a sight for young women," Eamon said.

I shot him a withering look. "I'll be the one to decide that. What's happened?" I repeated.

Eamon stepped back with a shrug of his shoulders, clearly put out. "Christine is dead. She's lying in there with blood all over her. Don't say I didn't warn you. We can't have everyone screaming the place down," he grumbled. "When I was passing by, I saw Lorna knocking on Christine's door. She told me she wanted to check on Christine because of some disturbance last night. She knocked, and when she didn't get any response, I made the decision to use a bit of force to break the lock." He puffed himself up with what I thought was probably pride. "It was locked from the inside, you see. Even if we'd had a key, we couldn't have got in. When I busted it open the key was in the lock on the other side of the door."

"Has anyone checked she's really dead? Or called the police?" I added, remembering that it was the proper thing to do. Not everyone had a limp and lifeless local lawman.

"I'd say she's dead as a doornail. If you're so keen, go and see for yourself," Eamon continued, standing there with his hands in his pockets.

I'd sure hate to be a female taking his university course! I thought. Eamon was one of those classic cases where a man believes he is being chivalrous, when really, he is being sexist.

I knew she was dead as soon as I entered the room.

Death had a particular silence and a particular smell. I looked to the left and saw Christine lying face down. Blood stained her back where something had clearly attacked her. Her eyes were shut and there was no grimace of pain on her face. Were it not for the blood, it would have been simple to believe she was still sleeping. Just in case, I checked her pulse. She was ice cold and stiff where rigor mortis had set in. Christine Montague had been dead for a while.

I looked around the room, gathering my thoughts. There was an alarm clock on the floor, the same as in my room. I realised it was displaying the wrong time. The hands showed half-past three, and the plastic front had been shattered. I hypothesised that it could have been one of the series of thumps I'd heard prior to Sylvia's scream when she'd seen a stranger in her room. There was a shattered mug on the floor and a puddle of liquid surrounding it and the tea bag in a sorry heap. I touched a finger to it but the tea was ice cold. It must have been the mug Christine had broken when she'd seen the spider.

"Oh. That's going to delay the day," Fergus said, coming up behind me and sharing some of his characteristically inappropriate wit. "What happened? It looks like she was stabbed in the back."

He walked over to the open window and looked out across the grounds. "Do you think an intruder came through here and killed her?"

I frowned. "What plausible reason have you got for that being the case?"

"Well… she is dead," Fergus began. "There could be a psycho on the loose. Perhaps they saw an opportunity and took it. Or, it was a robbery gone wrong. I don't know if you noticed, but Christine was wearing some pretty big rocks. Where are they now?"

I raised my eyebrows at him. "You can do better than that. You said it yourself - this place is locked down tight. You've never managed to break-in. Why would someone be able to do it now? I even asked Jack if that was possible last night after Sylvia saw that man in her room. He claimed there was no chance."

"Sylvia saw a man in her room?"

"I saw him too when he left and ran down the corridor. I saw someone anyway," I corrected, still not sure of exactly what I'd witnessed at that early hour. "I thought he was wearing some kind of military outfit." I was keeping the glowing nature of that outfit to myself for as long as possible. Fergus would have a field day if he caught wind of it!

My companion looked intrigued. "I did hear that this place has its fair share of paranormal phenomena. Perhaps you caught a glimpse of a ghost."

I looked back at the body on the bed. "It wasn't a ghost that did that to her." I bent down and looked as closely as I could at the blood on her back. The covers were off, and on closer inspection, it was clear that the source of the blood originated from the multiple wounds that had been made in her back. The wounds themselves were certainly unusual. They were round puncture wounds. There were so many of them, it was impossible to get a clear look at any one wound. It was obvious that something other than a standard knife had been use to inflict the damage. I looked around but nothing fitting that description had been left lying around in the room. There would probably have been a lot of blood left on the weapon, too.

"Did they get tired halfway through?" Fergus commented, coming closer and pointing to some of the shallower cuts. By contrast, there were some seriously deep punctures alongside them. "And they're so random. It's like a frenzy."

"That is strange," I agreed, having already noticed the haphazard nature of the attack.

"Maybe they switched hands," Fergus suggested, miming striking with one and then another. "Two weapons, two hands - one of them weaker than the other - and a whole lot of rage," he completed.

"You may be right," I conceded, knowing it would fit with the shallow and deep cut observations.

"Oh, jeez," Jack said, walking into the room and immediately back out again.

Fergus walked over to him, shielding the corpse from view. "Has anyone called the police?" he asked, reiterating my earlier question that had gone unanswered.

Jack took a couple of quick breaths. "No, we can't. We've got no contact with anyone until the timer runs out."

"What about sending someone out to get them? We can get outside, can't we?" Fergus pressed.

Jack nodded, but then shook his head. "Going outside is permitted. I think it even forms part of the course. It was on the itinerary map we were given when Lorna and I got the job. But this whole place is surrounded by some ridiculous fences. There are landmines, too! You can do that on private property. There is no way anyone is getting in or out. The outside is, like, super protected. Not cool, man."

"Don't you have an emergency phone? You must have been left with something?" I queried. Even a distress flare would be welcome right now.

Jack shook his head. "We said at the start of the course that there'd be no outside communication. When you handed in all of your phones and devices, that was that. We've got nothing either. It's part of the gimmick, yeah? A complete retreat from reality to learn flower arranging. We've got loads of first aid supplies and all that. Even if someone had been poisoned yesterday, it would have been totally fine."

"How reassuring," I said, not meaning it for a second. I looked down at the body and privately thought that no amount of first aid was going to bring Christine Montague back from the dead.

"So, what you're saying is… we've got to leave Christine like this for two more days before we can even attempt to contact the police," Fergus summarised, looking just as bemused as I felt. I understood the whole 'authentic retreat' thing, but who the heck didn't have a phone or some kind of method of communication, just in case the unthinkable happened? Even a carrier pigeon would have been better than what we had now, which was nothing. Nada. Zip.

"We could move her into a fridge or a freezer, or something," Jack said, displaying knowledge gleaned from too many films.

"No we can't. It's a crime scene. It's bad enough that everyone's already traipsed through here." I knew I was just as much to blame as the rest of them on this point, but someone had needed to check that Christine really was beyond help.

"Crime scene?" Jack suddenly looked very worried indeed.

"Come on, lad. She didn't stab herself," Fergus said, his mouth tweaking up with bitter humour. "Someone killed her… and my money is on it being one of the lot we're locked in here with. We're trapped here with a killer. For all we know, they could strike again."

"Fergus!" I said, horrified that he was putting ideas into the impressionable guide's head. It was obvious that Jack was traumatised by this incident and he was only going to make it worse.

"You mean it's murder? There's a murderer here?" Jack looked like he might be about to faint or run.

"It is probable that someone amongst us is responsible for

Christine's death. That is, unless there is someone else here with us that we don't know about?" I waited for a beat in case Jack knew something that Fergus and I didn't. No special surprise guests were lurking around here.

I'd wondered if Christine could have been an actress hired to fake her own death in a strange murder-mystery twist to this extreme flower arranging thing. The whole day could have been focused on funeral flower arranging - which was definitely an art form unto itself. I'd quickly dismissed that idea when I'd got close enough to smell the blood and had felt the cool flesh that couldn't be faked. I was still wondering if I was the morbid one having ideas like that.

"However..." I continued, wanting to calm Jack down from the state Fergus was working him up into "...I'm sure that there's a motive for the events that occurred here last night. Someone must know something about it. It could be that there is someone on this course who had a past with Christine that they haven't shared with anyone else." I considered. "She's a pretty big name in the garden design world... from what she was saying, at least. I think Tanya knew who she was prior to this course." I was remembering back to our introductions and the way she'd shot sideways looks at Christine, hoping for approval.

"Rich works for her. He probably did it," Fergus decided.

"Fergus!" I protested, annoyed all over again. "It's important that we don't throw around baseless allegations," I said for Fergus' benefit as well as Jack's. This was fast spiralling out of my control. If the hysteria spread, then where would we be?

"Then what do we do?" Jack said, looking from me to Fergus with wide eyes.

"We start asking questions," Fergus said saying the first sensible thing I'd heard from him so far today. "We've got two more days before we can get out of here. The main thing now is to keep ourselves safe, in case it is a homicidal maniac. Diana thinks there's a motive for this murder, so we should probably figure out what it is. At the very least, if we find one, it will let us know that the rest of us probably aren't in any danger."

"Are you going to try to solve the crime? My dad always said you were a really good investigator. You should take the case! The scene of the crime won't be fresh when the police do arrive. Plus, someone could easily tamper with the evidence before then." Jack's eyes were shining again.

"I suppose I could give it a whirl..." Fergus said thoughtfully.

I cleared my throat. "Tampering with evidence is a bad idea." Not that I'd been excellent at following that rule in the past. But those had been an entirely different set of circumstances! The glint in Fergus' eye hinted he was thinking the same thing. Fergus and I shared a secret that neither of us could ever tell.

"I wouldn't be tampering with it. I'd be looking at it. Diana, you're a scientist, what do you see in front of you?" Fergus held out his hands, full of drama.

"I see a mess that's best left for the police," I replied, a trifle primly. Fergus kept his hands outstretched and my eyes caught on something sticking out from underneath the bed. I reached down and gingerly drew out a hastily tied posy of wilted snapdragons. Their peach petals looked sad and unloved and I could tell they'd been without water for a while. However, it wasn't enough to cover up the fact that something had been written in a slim marker pen on the back of the delicate petals. I squinted at the wilting plant and could just make out one remaining word - Harving. If there had been more writing originally, I couldn't make it out.

I placed the flowers on the nightstand and heard my foot

crunch on something on the floor. Looking down, I discovered an ornate hair pin with a jewel flower was lying there.

"Hey, look…" Fergus was bent down by the bed with a finger extended. I followed where he was pointing and discovered there was a medical bracelet on the floor - the kind you have if you're allergic to something, or need special care should anything happen to you.

"I don't believe it," I said, looking from the medical bracelet to the hair pin and then back to the snapdragons.

"What's up?" Jack asked.

"It's all too convenient," I explained. "Someone has been murdered, and now we're finding clues all over the place. This feels far too much like a set up."

"Maybe the murderer made some mistakes?" Jack suggested, but I wasn't willing to believe it was that easy.

I wrinkled my nose, finally becoming aware of a bitter scent that had been on my periphery for a while. "What is that?" I muttered and followed the scent over to the smashed cup of tea. I sniffed and thought I could smell chai tea mixed with something I couldn't identify. The bag was full of twigs and bits, but I believed that was just the way chai looked.

"Does anyone know if there's any herbal tea in the kitchen cupboards?" I asked.

"Nope, nothing like that. There's just English Breakfast, green tea, and filter coffee," Fergus said with confidence. I threw him a questioning look. "When you were settling into the room yesterday, I went looking in case I needed a snack later," he explained.

"I suppose someone could have brought their own tea bags with them," I mused.

"Look at the time!" Jack said, bringing his hands up to his face. "We've got to start the challenges for the day, or we won't finish in time!"

Fergus and I looked at him.

"Jack, someone's been murdered. Continuing with the course is…" I started to say.

"…essential!" Jack said, paling a little. "We have to carry on. This whole thing is designed to create a high pressure, high risk, high reward learning environment in order to stimulate the formation of new neurological pathways."

Fergus looked blank.

"He means bad things are going to happen if we don't finish the course," I translated.

Jack nodded.

We walked out of the room containing Christine's corpse. I silently pocketed the hair pin, which I'd trodden on anyway. I noticed Fergus palm the medical bracelet. It would appear that despite what we'd said about obvious clues and not tampering with the evidence, neither of us were willing to let it drop so easily.

"Is Christine really dead?" Rich asked once we were outside and in the midst of the gathered group, who'd all been waiting outside of the room.

"It's true," I told them. "It would appear that she has been murdered. There are several wounds to her back and no sign of the weapon that inflicted them. If everyone could keep their eyes open for something that could be used to make a round puncture wound, that would be great." I used my finger and thumb to indicate the approximate size of the implement used.

"Murdered?" Duncan reached out to clutch his wife's shoulders. "I thought no one could get in here? How has she been murdered?"

"Diana thinks one of us did it," Rich said, looking at me with quiet amusement. I wasn't sure what he found funny about the situation. Surely he had to know that he was suspect number one?

There was a stunned silence. Everyone markedly moved away from everyone else.

"I must have been the one to see her last. I, uh, knocked on her door because I wanted to tell her how much of an inspiration she was to me. I'm a nobody when it comes to garden design. Christine is such an icon," Tanya muttered.

"What time was that?" I asked.

"Oh, heavens! Probably about ten? She wasn't that happy to see me, if truth be told, but she was alive." Tanya bit her lip. "I should have known. She was brilliant, but she had a reputation for not sharing any of her secrets with anyone."

People were still backing away from one another. I decided someone had to intervene. "There is no need for anyone to panic. At the moment, the best course of action is to follow the instructions of our guides. Jack has informed us that we must continue with these challenges, or face some pretty bad consequences. It's the way this course has been designed. Unfortunately, with no contact with the outside world, there is nothing we can do to avoid continuing."

"We're already late," Jack chimed in, looking desperately at Lorna, who was still a greenish colour.

We all heard the alarm sound in the food hall. A voice boomed out over hidden speakers. "The early bird gets the worm! The late flower arranger gets a lesson about flower-choice…"

"What?!" Eamon said before everyone clamped their hands over their noses. The most terrible, pungent smell had suddenly wafted through the living quarters.

"What is that?" Bella managed before clamping her hand over her mouth, too. Apparently you could taste it as well as smell it.

"That is the potent scent of the corpse lily, or Rafflesia arnoldii," the hidden voice announced. "This particular flower uses its pungent scent to draw flies and insects that usually lay their eggs in rotting materials. The scent mimicry tricks the insects into pollinating the plant, thus continuing its survival. It is very unlikely that you will come across any members of this distinctive genus of flowers during your future flower arranging, but I hope this will serve as a reminder that scent matters. Always consider your flowers and the scents they will create. Not all blooms smell sweet."

"The first challenge! We've got to go," Jack said, and then looked like he might be about to be sick.

No one argued when he and Lorna led the way into a room leading off the food hall and slammed the door behind us. Cool, clear air suddenly filled the space and everyone breathed a collective sigh of relief. It was only then that I realised half of the group were still dressed in pyjamas. I was wearing the same clothes I'd worn yesterday- having gone to bed in them after learning Fergus was sharing my room.

There was no time to dwell on it as the screen flashed on and we were greeted by Emilia's smiling face. "Good morning everyone! I trust you slept well and enjoyed the breakfast of local produce? All sourced from a farm just down the road from here," she said, so inappropriately it was unreal. I could almost hear the sounds of stomachs grumbling as we all collectively realised we'd skipped breakfast. I hoped there'd be a coffee break.

"Today we will be focusing on your seasonal knowledge of flowers and foraging. A lot of you will be familiar with imported blooms, but did you know that many fantastic flowers and foliage can be found on our very own British Isles? All you have to keep in mind is seasonality and sustainability. In this first challenge, you will be presented with a menu of flowers. As a group, you must pick all of the flowers which are in season in the UK during the month of March. Only when you have selected all of the flowers will the door open and the challenge be complete. You may use the reading material in this room to help you, but this challenge is about shared knowledge. Work together to discuss choices and I'm sure you'll succeed. Make a wrong choice..." Emilia smiled a little ruefully. "...and you'll discover a flower arranger's bane. Good luck!" Her smiling face faded and in its place was a screen full of images of flowers and their latin and common names listed below.

"There must be a hundred of them!" Bella said, voicing everyone's thoughts aloud.

"How about we start by discussing the ones we already know?" I suggested, deciding that someone should step up. "We are looking for flowers that bloom in March. I know that primroses, Queen Anne's lace, and lily of the valley are all spring blooms and would definitely be around during March. Are we all in agreement?" Most of the group nodded. When no one contradicted me, I stepped forwards and tapped the three flower icons. They disappeared with a cheerful 'bing'.

"Well done!" a congratulatory voice said each time.

"I know a few..." Lady Isabella added before quietly saying her suggestions. After some brief discussion, these, too, were tapped and disappeared. Next, Sylvia contributed, as did the rest of the group. Bella surprised me by being adamant about paphiopedilum orchids - something I hadn't even heard of prior to now. Neither had anyone else, but she was certain that she'd always seen them flowering right before Easter when she'd been a child running round her grandma's greenhouse. We'd held our breaths when she'd pressed the exotic looking icon, but there'd been the familiar bing and 'well done'.

"Looks like we might have some research to do," Eamon reluctantly acknowledged as we all looked at the remaining icons on the screen. We'd made some good progress but there was still a large number of images on the screen. I had a feeling this challenge had been designed with some tricky flowers to throw even those with a lot of prior experience. We all dutifully walked over to the corner of the room and selected some likely looking books. Soon, everyone was reading whilst raising their heads to occasionally check their findings against the board.

Everyone apart from Fergus.

"Don't!" I warned when I saw exactly what he was about to do.

"How hard can it be…" he muttered and selected a picture at random.

The cheery voice said "Well done!"

Fergus grinned and tried again.

This time his choice flashed red and a warning siren sounded, loudly alerting the group to what one of their number had just done.

"Whoops!" Fergus said, shrugging his shoulders with a guilty grin on his face. With a sudden 'whoosh' sound an entire bucket of glitter was emptied through the grate directly above where he was standing, just in front of the screen. For a moment, everyone marvelled at the gold and sparkly figure in front of them. Fergus coughed and spat some glitter out. "Probably should have kept my mouth closed…" he muttered, looking down at himself.

In spite of the traumatic events of the morning, I found myself grinning. "Glitter… a flower arranger's bane. That's clever."

"They used adhesive," Fergus complained, trying and failing to brush the stuff off himself. "I'm going to stay glittery until we can get back to the showers."

"Let that be a lesson to you," Lady Isabella airily commented, whilst still browsing one of the books. I raised my eyebrows at Fergus. I wasn't the only one who thought he was behaving like an ass.

"When are we going to discuss what happened to poor Christine?" Eamon broke the silence when we'd all ground to a halt on our flower research and the door still hadn't opened.

"What is there to discuss? She's dead. We can't do anything for her," Rich said with a shrug so casual I immediately wondered if he'd seized the opportunity to get rid of a boss he didn't like. He looked over at me and silently shook his head, his grin growing wider. He knew what I was thinking.

"Yes, but someone here probably killed her. That's the consensus, isn't it?" Eamon continued, regarding Rich with the same suspicion I felt.

"We don't know that for sure, someone could have broken in," Rich suggested, playing devil's advocate.

"They can't..." Jack started to say even as Rich continued.

"...Or someone else is in here with us. We're not allowed free run of the bunker. Who knows who might be creeping around? Perhaps this was a set-up all along for some twisted person to pick us all off one by one whilst we're here completely cut off from the world." He rubbed his chin thoughtfully. "It would be like hunting heaven for a serial killer."

There was a shocked silence.

"I think it's far more likely that there is a personal motive for this murder. One we don't yet know," I said, hoping to stop this runaway train before it picked up speed. Hysteria was the last thing we needed on a 'high stakes' course where working together was the key. The course creator had already made us risk food poisoning on the first day. I suspected things were only going to get worse.

"What motive could someone possibly have for killing her? We've only known each other for a day! Apart from

Rich." Eamon looked speculatively at the young PR man again.

Rich picked an imaginary spot of dirt from his finger-nails. "Trust me, I'd have killed her long ago if I'd decided I wanted to be done with my boss. The pay packet made her worth putting up with, but I'd be the first to admit that she wasn't easy to get along with. Christine got where she was by being ruthless and having an angle no one else had. I wouldn't like to be in her shoes, should there be any moral reckoning in the great beyond." Rich shrugged his shoulders. "But that just means she had enemies. Maybe one of them is here right now and hiding it from us. I still think it's a psycho. This whole course is pretty messed up, isn't it? Who's to say someone didn't plan this whole thing to take us all out? This weirdo might love violence. Stabbing one of us dead whilst we were sleeping could be how this guy gets his fun."

"Christine wasn't actually stabbed to death. Or at least... she was already dead when the stabbing happened," I said, deciding to share something I'd observed in the hopes that it might shock the truth out of someone in the group.

Everyone stared at me.

"She was poisoned. It's been bugging me ever since I smelled something bitter in her room. I thought it could be the cup of herbal tea that got smashed, but there isn't any tea of that kind in the cupboards here. And the bitter smell suggests poison - and a natural one at that."

"She could have brought her own tea with her. It could have already been poisoned by someone before this course," Bella suggested, expanding on my own thoughts from earlier.

"You could be right, but I think there is more than enough evidence that suggests that this crime was committed by someone here, or someone who has access to us. The most obvious thing is that someone stabbed her - perhaps believing that they were killing Christine, or just making sure she was really dead. But the writing on the petals of a wilted bunch of snapdragons I found under her bed is more indicative - especially as they were the same kind of snapdragons we were working with yesterday."

"You saw writing on a flower?" Duncan looked baffled, and he wasn't alone.

"It was a name. That, too, had taken some thinking about before I'd remembered why it sounded familiar. The name was Harving." I looked up and saw recognition echo round the group. Everyone had heard of Elliot Harving - whether they were interested in floriculture or not.

"Wasn't he the designer that died at Chelsea?" Fergus said, screwing his face up at the memory.

"It was a terrible accident," Tanya commented, looking saddened. "I was working on a different garden at the show on that day, but everyone there knew about it."

Fergus looked thoughtful. "The way I heard it, it might not have been an accident at all. There were claims that the whole thing was an act of sabotage."

Trust Fergus to know the conspiracy theory version, I silently thought.

"Sorry, but what happened?" Duncan asked, looking around the room at all the grave faces.

It was Tanya who answered his question. "Elliot Harving was an up and coming designer. He was tipped to take gold during his first ever year at Chelsea Flower Show in the show garden category. The centrepiece of his design, which I believe was entitled 'A Rust for Life', was this big aged steel sculpture. His whole garden was full of scrap metal. It just blended so well with his plant choices..." She shook her head at the memory. "When people went to see it for the first time at an exclusive pre-judging viewing the sculpture collapsed. I think witnesses said that Elliot saved a lot of people. He saw it start to fall and ran at the crowd, telling them to get back. No one else was seriously hurt, but the sculpture crushed Elliot. The entire nation of gardeners mourned his loss."

"People were arrested for it, weren't they? Wasn't it the sculptors themselves who were found negligent?" Sylvia chirped up. There were sounds of agreement.

Eamon shook his head. "What on earth does any of this have to do with Christine? Elliot's death was tragic, but the perpetrators were punished ages ago. It's all done and dusted."

"I think the writing on the snapdragon is evidence to the contrary," I said, pausing for a second while I thought. "And for some reason, the writer wanted Christine Montague to see it before she died."

6

THE DEVIL IS IN THE DETAILS

E yes darted to and fro around the room.
   "I didn't do it," Rich said when the eyes kept
   coming back to him - a man who hadn't exactly
spoken highly of his boss.

"Well, one of us probably did!" Eamon batted back,
folding his arms and looking around the room.

"Luckily, we have a professional investigator amongst us!"
Jack piped up before gesturing grandly at Fergus.

Everyone looked at him. They didn't look convinced. "I
thought he was some conspiracy nut..." I heard someone say,
although I wasn't able to pinpoint the person.

"I have been known to investigate mysteries. The thing to
keep in mind is that I don't have anything to do with flowers.
So, you can say with near certainty that I would have had no
reason to kill Christine. I was asleep all night, wasn't I?" He
looked at me questioningly.

I sighed when the attention was once more focused on
me. "He's a heavy sleeper." I did my best to ignore the curious
looks Rich was shooting from me to Fergus. He could
wonder all he wanted.

"We were asleep all night, too, weren't we, darling?" Duncan said, looking at his wife.

She nodded silently.

"That's hardly fair - you four claiming alibis by using one another. For all we know, either pair of you could have worked together!" Eamon protested. The lecturer was starting to become a thorn in my side. He took a step forwards so that he was standing in front of the screen and at the centre of attention. "What we should do is keep an eye out and keep our distance. If no one is friendly to anyone, any person trying to get close to you will be exceedingly suspicious."

"But what if the killer broke in and isn't one of us at all?" Rich persisted.

Eamon threw his hands up in the air. "Well dash it all! Do what you like. All I know is that I certainly didn't kill her. I'm a lecturer! I have a reputation to uphold. This whole thing is preposterous!" He brought his hands back down, accidentally brushing a hand against the screen. The siren sounded and glitter - this time blue - was dumped over Eamon. "Dash it all!" he repeated turning around and pressing another one of the icons at random, fury taking over. "Well done! Challenge completed!" the voice announced and the door slid open. Two peeved glitter-covered men stalked through the doorway to find out what awaited us whilst the rest of us trailed miserably behind them.

I found myself biting my lip. It was clear that nobody was going to accept anyone else's authority on this matter, because no one trusted anyone. Whilst that was a reasonable decision to have made, it didn't make getting any closer to figuring out who killed Christine Montague, and why, an easy task. *The first thing to do is to work out why Elliot Harving's name was written on that flower,* I thought, wondering what kind of connection Christine could have had to him and why someone had bothered to write it on a petal. *And why a snapdragon?* Just before I walked over the threshold, I hesitated, remembering the title of one of the books that had been in amongst the research. I ran back and grabbed it before following the group through the doorway and down the corridor beyond.

"Ah! Some fresh air at last," I heard Eamon say. A second later I saw light bloom at the end of the tunnel.

I shoved the slim book into the pocket of my garden overalls that I'd worn yesterday and always wore when working with flowers. The book curled up a bit, but with the internet out, it was my only opportunity to do some research to discover if my suspicions were correct.

I walked out of the long tunnel into the daylight beyond. This next challenge, whatever it was, would take place outside in the grounds.

"This way!" Jack called, beckoning the trailing group towards what looked like a lean-to wood store, built close to the edge of a wood.

Within the store there was a sealed off shed area. A small screen flickered on just above the door. "Hello everyone!" Damien, our virtual teacher, greeted us. "You've already learned about the importance of using seasonal plants and flowers in your arrangements today. It is excellent knowledge to possess for sustainability of the environment, in order to avoid unnecessary shipping from overseas, and also for your wallet. In season is cheaper! Now, some of you will still have to contend with brides who 'know what they want' but it is something to think about, and it will help you to plan your arrangements ahead of time, knowing what will be around when you're arranging them. Today you will learn to make use of a very old skill - foraging! In our beautiful

British Isles there are a few rules that must be abided by when you are out in public. No picking of wild flowers! However, that doesn't extend to greenery or anything else interesting you might be able to get your hands on. As you know, we are on private land at the moment, so everything is up for grabs. All we ask is that you source your foraged items with an eye for sustainability. Pick, cut, and dig thoughtfully, with a mind to always leaving enough behind for regeneration. Your guides will now show you your tools for this challenge... and then off and away! You have two and a half hours to forage and create ten displays worthy of a wild crown."

"Ten displays," I muttered, remembering that these messages had been recorded prior to Christine's death. We were going to be short of an arrangement. I forgot all about that conundrum when Lorna opened the door to the shed and revealed our foraging gear.

As soon as the door was open, my eyes had drifted to the row of trowels and miniature garden forks hanging along a shelf. There was a space where the tenth fork should have been. I looked around the group to see if anyone looked particularly worried or shady, but no one seemed to have even noticed the missing fork. No one apart from Fergus who was mouthing 'it's a fork!' at me from across the other side of the group. I mouthed back 'I know!' and then added 'Be quiet!' for good measure.

"Right! Everyone grab yourselves anything you think you'll need. There are ten hammered metal pails in here. That's where we're supposed to display the final pieces. The actual display shelf is here," Jack said, pointing to a plank of wood clearly marked 'display shelf'.

I found myself wondering once again how much more the guides really knew than their charges. They seemed as in the dark as we were about the content of the challenges. I privately thought they'd been employed to add drama and act as people shepherds. They simply had to make sure everyone went to the right places. But today they'd need to step it up a notch.

"Lorna and Jack... we're going to need another arrangement. One of you will have to take Christine's place," I said in amongst the gear grab in progress.

"Oh, yes... right, of course," Jack said, looking frazzled.

"I'll do it," Lorna said. I noticed she still looked green around the gills. Perhaps the fresh air and foraging would take her mind off what she'd seen this morning.

"Let's share a fork," Fergus said in my ear. "Then perhaps no one will notice the missing one."

"Where do you think it is?" I said. The fork wasn't hanging up, and it hadn't been left in the room with Christine. So where the heck was it?

I couldn't believe I hadn't realised what had caused the holes in Christine's back from the very start, but I'd been thrown off by the sheer number of puncture wounds. I hadn't noticed that three of them must have been in perfect alignment every time. A miniature garden fork was exactly the right size to have done the job. If we could find the one missing from the toolshed lineup, I was certain we'd have our murder weapon.

"If I catch anyone sneaking up on me... it will be the worst for you!" Eamon told the group whilst waving a pair of garden shears in a threatening manner. No one else made any threats, but I could tell that our group's trust building had taken several leaps backwards today.

Fergus and I walked through the woods for five minutes carrying our pails without stopping to look at any of the interesting flowers, twigs, and leaves along the way. When we were finally far enough away to not be able to hear any sounds of the others following behind, Fergus stopped walking and turned to me. "So... what are we going to do?"

I lifted my shoulders up and let them down again. "What is there to do? The sensible thing is to keep our heads down for the last day and a bit and then hand over everything we know to the police, once we get out."

Fergus shook his head. "The police aren't going to find anything! Just look at the clues we found in the room. You said it yourself - they're too obvious. They were almost certainly left there to frame one person or another. That or the robber liked sparkly flower hair pins and had a medical condition. But I think that there's no way that this murder was committed on impulse. Christine came to me the day before she was killed. She knew someone was after her."

"The snapdragons. I wonder if they were in her room from the start?" I mused, giving Rich Strauss' theory about the course provider being in on it a little more credence.

Fergus shook his head. "I think someone wanted her scared. They could have easily sneaked off into her room before she took her baggage there. We all sort of drifted around before we ate, didn't we? Could you say with absolute certainty that everyone was present? Did anyone pop off to the loo? Our rooms were marked with our names. The only thing I can't figure out is why would the killer want to warn her?"

"Because they knew there was nothing she could do to escape it. We're all stuck in here with each other. Where could she run? They wanted her to know her time was up and they wanted her to know the reason why," I said, realising it must be true. "We have to find out exactly what happened to Elliot Harving. I think someone here knows. And someone here knows how Christine Montague ties in with it all."

Fergus grinned, twirling the shared fork in his hand.

"That sounds a lot like you're planning to do some asking around instead of waiting for the police."

I frowned, realising the truth of his words. "The police won't understand. I don't know if they'll even look beyond an opportunistic and sadistic robber. The snapdragon evidence is gone by now. There's only our word for it." I bit my lip. "In fact, I'm not sure that the killer intended anyone other than Christine to spot their hidden message after she'd received it. Snapdragons wilt fast when left out of water. If her window hadn't been left open, the temperature would have been warm enough to make the petals wilt so much I probably wouldn't have even noticed it." I thought about it. "I think it might be the only genuine clue we have so far."

Fergus nodded. "We were meant to find the hair pin and the medical bracelet... but not the flower and writing. That would make sense. However, it doesn't mean that they aren't still clues. Especially if we know more than the killer intended us to find out." He pulled the medical bracelet out of his pocket. I would have criticised him, had I not still been holding onto the hair pin. With the scene of the crime hardly on lockdown it had seemed natural for us to hold onto these key pieces of 'evidence'. Either they would have remained in place, and therefore been deliberately planted to tip the police in the wrong direction, or they'd have mysteriously vanished before we were released. In which case, they couldn't have been brought to bear as evidence. I reassured myself that we'd done the only thing we could, given the circumstances.

"This thing is so old that most of the details are worn off. I can't make out a name, but I think it's for someone who's diabetic. I'm not even sure if it's a man or a woman's," Fergus said, looking thoughtfully at the shining metal before returning it to his pocket. "Shouldn't be too hard to figure out who it belongs to, right?"

"It is a good place to start," I confessed, privately thinking the hair pin was also quite traceable. I remembered Lady Isabella wearing several diamanté hair pins on the day we'd all met. Could the flower pin be one of hers? Or was it one of the other floral-minded women on this course who'd dropped it? It could even have belonged to Christine. I dismissed the thought immediately. She'd preferred statement pieces. The pin was far too subtle for her tastes. I bit my lip. I would have to do some casual asking around. If it really was a genuine clue, with a bit of luck, the owner wouldn't realise they'd dropped it - or, more importantly, where they'd dropped it.

"Hey... earlier you said that Christine was poisoned by her tea. What exactly did you mean?" Fergus asked, poking at a bit of twig sticking out of the ground. I took his cue and started gathering greenery - it would be foolish to forget that we were being timed.

"I'm almost certain that she was poisoned. When I walked into the room, I smelled something bitter. Natural poisons are often accompanied by a bitter taste. It's the plant's way of warning you that it shouldn't be eaten. Secondly, I'm not a forensic pathologist, so I can't say for certain, but although it looked like there was a lot of blood at the scene, I don't think there actually was that much - at least, not as much as there would have been if Christine's heart had still been pumping blood around her body when she was stabbed."

Fergus goggled as he thought it over. "The police will know that, right? They'll be able to tell she was poisoned first?"

I tilted my head from side to side. "That would depend on how closely they look. When you see stab-wounds and blood, you tend to make an assumption." I frowned, thinking of the cup of tea. "I only knew because of the smell of the stuff. We probably should have made sure no one touched the tea bag or cleared up the tea. It's evidence."

"Why would someone kill her twice?" Fergus marvelled, seizing a giant stem and pulling hard.

"I think they didn't want to have a fight on their hands." I looked at the fork in Fergus' hand. "If you're not a professional killer, and I really don't think the person responsible for this is, you wouldn't want to take any chances. Could you guarantee that you'd kill someone with your first strike of that fork? You saw the way not all of the strikes penetrated the skin. The attack was full of rage, but not skill."

Fergus kept on pulling up his leaves whilst I considered everything we knew and everything that we didn't.

I suddenly focused on what my foraging partner was actually doing.

"Fergus! That's giant hogweed!" I said, horrified to discover exactly what he was yanking on.

Fergus released the plant and looked down at his hand. "Is that bad? I thought it looked nice and big. I was going to bung a few in the pail and call it an arrangement."

"I'm sure you'd have got points for audacity and insanity," I said, glancing anxiously up at the sun and then back down at Fergus' hands. "You used both hands? Just your hands?" I asked. He nodded. After looking around for inspiration, I was forced to take off my overalls and wrap them around his hands. "Be careful with that. There's a book in one of the pockets."

"Why the hand wrap?" Fergus queried, looking faintly amused by my reaction. He wouldn't be amused if I'd already acted too late.

"Giant hogweed strips away the skin's natural protection against sunlight. You should only touch it whilst wearing protective gear, and even then, if any gets on your skin... it's bad. Once exposed to sunlight the skin will blister horrifically. If we can avoid that happening, it would be great. Let's find some water. You need to wash it off as much as you can. Then, we'd better hope someone carries factor 99 suncream with them... or gardening gloves." I thought I knew which was more likely given the season. Fergus was going to have to put up with the pair of gloves I'd brought with me, just in case. My only concern was that they wouldn't go far enough up his wrists to protect him properly.

In the end, we found a solution. On the way back inside to attempt to find some water along the approved route to our nearest facilities we bumped into Lady Isabella Duprix. After explaining what had befallen Fergus, she'd sympathised and had pulled a couple of long formal gloves out of the little handbag she carried everywhere with her. "You just never know when you might need to dress for the occasion," she informed us before reassuring Fergus that they weren't her best pair and that she didn't need them back.

"Before I forget, I found a hairpin this morning. Does it belong to you?" I asked, hoping I was being subtle. I pulled the pin out from my trouser pocket and showed it to her. She inspected it warily before shaking her head. "That's not mine. Perhaps it belongs to one of the other ladies. Or maybe it was Christine's," she added, making me believe she'd seen straight through my casual questioning.

"I don't suppose you're diabetic, are you?" Fergus pitched in, abandoning subtlety entirely.

"I am not," Lady Isabella told him shortly. "I think we should all be returning to our foraging. There can't be long left, and you know the things they do when you're late." She looked sickened by the memory of the terrible smell we'd all been subjected to that morning. I dearly hoped it would have been fumigated by the time we returned to our sleeping quarters. *Although, no one can do anything about the body next door,* I silently remembered, realising that I would be sleeping two doors down from death tonight.

"Thanks for the gloves," Fergus said before walking off towards the woods.

I hesitated for a moment, some part of me knowing this would be one of only a few chances I'd have to speak to another course member alone and not be overheard. "How did you hear about the accident with Elliot Harving?" I asked.

Lady Isabella blinked. "It was all over the papers. I was due to go to Chelsea the day after. No one had much cheer after it. It was a terrible tragedy for that poor young man. When they found the sculptors responsible for negligence and threw the book at them it didn't much feel like justice for anyone. I don't know much about sculpting, but surely they made the sculpture to his designs? He would have checked it himself. I just don't see how it was the sculptors' fault, that's all." She gave her head a gentle shake. "Did you hear what actually happened to the couple who made it? They were sent to prison! It just doesn't seem fair, does it? Not when people who have done far worse seem to get away with a slap on the wrist. I suppose it's all about who the press decides are the enemy - and they really went after those poor sculptors. It wasn't just their freedom that was taken, but their whole lives, their business, everything. Imagine working on something for your entire life and then 'poof!' it goes up in smoke." She sighed. "I'm not taking anything away from the tragedy that occurred. I just believe that the authorities could have shown a little more compassion in their convictions."

She looked down at the bunch of twigs augmented with some bright autumn berries and even a flower or two of a variety that I didn't recognise. "I think I've nearly finished my arrangement. I might go and get it judged. Good luck with yours." Lady Isabella gave me a curt nod before sweeping off in the direction of the toolshed.

"Learn anything interesting?" Fergus asked when I walked over to him and we began gathering twigs, leaves, and anything else we could get our hands on, in earnest.

"I don't think so," I confessed. "I think just about everyone on this course knows a reasonable amount about Elliot Harving, but I've no idea why his name was written on the snapdragon." I sucked on my bottom lip for a second. "I suppose I'll have to do some more asking around and see if anyone lets anything slip, but if we push too hard, we could end up ostracised from the group."

Fergus shrugged. "If anyone seems particularly unwilling to talk, you've probably found the guilty one. On the plus side, no one can really get away from you here."

"And on the minus side, we can't get away from the killer," I pointed out, wondering if it was wise to poke a stick into what might turn out to be a hornet's nest.

Fergus nodded, inspecting his gloved hands. "You know… these may be a little small, but boy, do I feel fancy!"

I rolled my eyes to the heavens and dumped some sloe-laden blackthorn stems into my pail. Finding the truth was going to be even harder with Fergus distracting me every few seconds.

"Let's get this challenge done and then think about our next move," I said, placing some twigs in his pail. "Perhaps something will turn up…"

At lunchtime, it did.

Everyone was sitting down to eat a lunch of smoked salmon sandwiches when we heard the scream. A quick scan of the table revealed that Sylvia was missing from the group.

"I'll go," I said, sliding out of my chair.

Rich slid out of his own at the same time. We looked at each other for a long moment. "Together?" he suggested, and I nodded.

We walked out of the dining hall towards the bedrooms to find out what had happened to Sylvia.

7

UNRAVELLING THE THREADS

S ylvia stood outside of her room with a shaking hand covering her heart.

"Are you all right?" I asked, wondering if there was a medical emergency that needed dealing with.

"No, dear, but I'm sure I will be soon. I just need a moment." She took a couple of deep breaths and some of the colour returned to her cheeks. "I popped into my room to freshen up and have a few moments to myself. I had to spend the whole morning in my night dress, you know, after that terrible stench and being forced to keep on with all of this after what happened to poor Christine. I reached into my knitting bag and felt something sticky. I thought that maybe a toffee had escaped, but when I looked at my hand, it was all red! I felt quite dizzy, dear, thinking I'd cut myself. But it was worse than that. When I looked inside the bag there was a hand fork in there, and it was absolutely covered in blood." She turned pale again. "I shan't be able to knit again! I certainly want that bag gone from my sight for good."

"Try not to worry. I'm sure you'll get a fresh supply of

wool once we're out of here and be back knitting in no time," I reassured her, knowing she was focusing on that issue to take her mind off the terrible truth - she had found the weapon used to stab Christine Montague.

Rich returned from Sylvia's room with the bloodstained knitting bag clutched between his thumb and forefinger. I considered the potential for him having tampered with the evidence before I let it go. This whole situation was a disaster when it came to crime scene preservation. Refusing to touch a knitting bag containing a weapon used in a murder was ridiculous - especially when Sylvia had already inadvertently touched it.

"I told you I saw a man in my room last night. He must have come in and dropped the fork. Maybe I scared him when I screamed," Sylvia said, looking more animated now that Rich and the bag were with us. I thought she was recovering well from the initial shock of her discovery. "No one believed me, but I was right! I knew I wasn't dreaming. He must have come in through the window and then run out through the door by unlocking it from the inside. I was so sure I locked it, you know, but I did leave the key in."

"Why would he run inside the bunker?" Rich asked, looking perplexed.

"Heaven knows! This place is huge. I'm sure there are simply hundreds of places to hide. You said yourself that this whole thing could be preconceived," Sylvia reminded him.

Rich shrugged it away. "I was probably a little overexcited when I said that. Do you remember what the man looked like?"

Sylvia went quiet for a moment. "Well, no. It was dark and I'd only just woken up. He was broader shouldered than you are. He wasn't as tall as Eamon, and he seemed to me to be slim - unlike Duncan. I may not have been able to see his face, but I'm quite certain I'd never seen that man before in my life. You probably saw him better than I did, Diana. What did you think?"

"You saw someone?" Rich looked surprised.

I nodded grudgingly, knowing that my story sounded pretty ridiculous. "The person was dressed in a military uniform from what I could see, and they were…ah…glowing. I didn't see anything apart from their back as they ran down the corridor." I pointed in the direction I'd watched the person run. "I didn't see where they went, but Jack said it's a dead end down there. So, either they walked through a locked door, or they went back into one of our rooms." I left the implication hanging.

"You didn't recognise the glowing military guy?" Rich enquired, looking faintly amused by the hint of accusation.

"No. Sylvia's description was perfect. I don't think it was you, Eamon, or Duncan… and Jack was right there a second later."

"You keep saying 'person'. You don't think it was a man?" Rich pressed.

I hesitated. "I'm not sure," I confessed. "All I know is that someone is playing a game with us - a game that has already resulted in a murder. And I don't think they've finished playing with us yet."

Rich was frowning. "I don't see how it has anything to do with any of us. It doesn't make any sense!"

"It doesn't make any sense at the moment," I corrected. "What do the both of you remember about what happened to Elliot Harving?"

Rich shook his head. "I still don't understand why you're asking about that random accident, but fine!" He raised his hands before I could say anything more. "I was working on the other side of the world when it happened, but it was news in all places where English-speaking people live. At the time, I was working for a construction company. I remember them all being shocked that the sculpture had collapsed. The media claimed it was to do with the old, unstable metal used, but the guys I worked with said it wasn't likely. Old steel that thick is tough - no matter how much rust is on it. The only way it would have collapsed would be a faulty weld or something deliberate that might have caused a weld to fail. In the end, I think they found there was some problem with the weld - just like my guys said. I reckon that was what got the sculptors in so much trouble. It was their responsibility to have done the proper job."

Sylvia nodded along. "I just felt sorry for the poor couple who went to prison over it all," she said, echoing Lady Isabella's sentiments. "I read in one of my gardening magazines that they later died. Both of them were taken ill whilst in there. I'm sure it's the sort of thing that could happen whether in prison or out of it, but you can't help thinking that for that couple - who I think were quite elderly - it must have been a terrible shock."

"Do either of you know why someone might think Christine was somehow involved in something to do with what happened to Elliot Harving?" I asked, feeling that I wasn't getting much closer to the truth. Everyone seemed to know about the story, but I couldn't find a single connection between Christine and the young man who had died... yet.

"No idea," Rich said, folding his arms and throwing me a skeptical look. "What about you? What do you know about Elliot Harving?" The look in his eye was clear: *What gives you the right to be asking all of the questions?*

I gave him a little shrug. "I don't actually remember much about the incident or the reports on it. I wasn't interested in anything to do with horticulture at the time. I was eating, sleeping, and breathing chemistry. My time was spent working at a laboratory in London."

"You said Christine was poisoned, right?" Rich clarified.

I inclined my head. "I believe she was drugged with a fatal dose of something. I think that it is likely she was dead by the time the attack occurred, but not being a pathologist, I can't stake a lot on that."

"I bet a chemist like you would know how to whip up some poison in no time at all."

I opened my mouth and shut it again. "I thought I'd already made it clear that the poison was likely from a natural source and not chemically obtained. But why on earth would I want to kill Christine Montague? I'm sure we can all agree that the attack was a frenzy of violence. It was done in hate." *But planned carefully in advance,* I silently added, believing it was the case. Someone had known that Christine Montague was going to be on this course, and someone had arranged for her to not make it out alive.

"You tell me," Rich batted back. "I've worked with Christine for long enough to know that there are no end of people she has rubbed the wrong way. You grow flowers, right? She could have slammed your work in her magazine column or blacklisted your company."

"I doubt it. I'm not exactly a big fish."

"Christine was spiteful. Don't underestimate the lengths she would go to if you did something, knowingly or otherwise, that might threaten her precious business."

I felt my forehead crease. "If you disliked her so much, why did you work for her?"

"I already told you. She paid me well for the privilege of my company and abilities. I'm not going to be picky about morals when that amount of cash is on the table." He winked at me.

"Are either of you diabetic?" I enquired, seeing as we were hardly tiptoeing around the matter now.

Both Sylvia and Rich shook their heads.

"I think Eamon is," Sylvia supplied, smiling sweetly at me.

Seeing as I still appeared to have Sylvia on my side, I directed the next question at her. "Do you know who might own this hair grip?" I pulled out the jewelled flower and showed it to her.

"I do! That is - it's mine. Wherever did you find it? I was looking for it before..." she paled again, remembering the fork in her knitting bag.

"It was on the floor next to Christine Montague's bed," I told her, wondering what it could mean. I'd thought that the obvious placement of the grip had been clumsy and Sylvia's easy admittance that it belonged to her was strange if she suspected that she might have lost it whilst committing murder.

"Well! I have no idea at all how it could have got there," the elderly lady said. I tried to imagine Sylvia shimmying out of the window, having just murdered Christine, and slipping back into her room by hauling herself up through her own window, having made sure to lock Christine's door from the inside... and then claiming she saw a man in her room. If it weren't for the fact that I'd witnessed the running figure with my own eyes and had seen Sylvia appear at the same time, I supposed I could have given the possibility more consideration, but aside from it sounding too crazy to be true, Sylvia struggled to climb up stairs. Dangling from windows was probably out of the question.

Then there was the bracelet to consider. If it did belong to Eamon, did that mean he was the killer? His figure didn't match that of the person I'd seen running away from Sylvia's room, but I knew better than to trust my own eyes - especially in the dark. With the right padding and a good costume, it could have been just about anyone running down that corridor.

Rich shook the bag and frowned before pulling it open and looking in. "Sylvia, are these your keys? There's a really big set in here."

"No, mine are in my handbag, dear," she told him, looking puzzled.

Rich pulled an apologetic face at me and then delved into the bag, pulling out a big jangling set and destroying another piece of evidence. There was a handy label attached that read 'Fennering Bunker Master Keys - Care of Jack Hart and Lorna Bates'.

"What could they have been doing in there?" Sylvia asked, her hand fluttering to her chest again.

"Oh, I don't know... maybe they were accidentally dropped in amongst all the wool when the killer was trying to dispose of the fork." Rich looked at me and raised his eyebrows. "I think you might be questioning the wrong group of people."

"Conspiring, are we?" Eamon said, walking towards us with a face like thunder.

"Not at all, Eamon. I had quite a fright after finding a garden fork covered in blood in my knitting bag. Diana and Rich kindly stayed with me until I was calm. We were just about to come back," Sylvia reassured him.

"Sure," Eamon said, looking unconvinced.

"You're diabetic, aren't you?" I asked, wanting to get to the bottom of this little mystery.

"Yes, what of it?" Eamon was more on guard than Sylvia had been, I noted, but then he would probably have been the same level of standoffish if I'd asked him something as simple as what colour the sky was today.

"Fergus just found a medical bracelet and wondered if it was yours. The name was worn off," I said, still wanting to see his reaction.

Eamon's hand went to his wrist. He frowned down at it. "Darn thing is always falling off at the slightest puff of air. I'll get it from him later. Kind of you to pick it up."

"No problem. It was lying next to Christine's bed," I said, dropping the truth on him the same way I had with Sylvia. I observed that I wasn't the only one in our little group watching the lecturer very closely.

Eamon immediately coloured. "Well, I! I went in to check what all the fuss was about, didn't I? I practically broke the door down," he stumbled. "It must have fallen off then. I do hope you're not suggesting…"

"…No one is suggesting anything," I finished, sensing that tempers were about to fly off the handle.

"What's going on?" Duncan and Bella arrived at our little group, looking almost as troubled as Eamon had.

"We found the weapon - a handheld garden fork - that we believe was used to stab Christine," I explained and then had to do so again when the rest of the dining group arrived outside Sylvia's room. We stood in a ring and looked round at one another in suspicion.

"Half an hour before we should start the next challenge," Jack's nervous voice came, trying to cut through the bad vibes, but our flower arranging circle was beyond that. Something needed to be done, or who knew what might happen next? Innocent people could be victimised and the real criminal might get away with a terrible crime. We had to approach this logically and calmly…

"I think an extraterrestrial was responsible for Christine's death," Fergus piped up.

I tried not to strangle him right there and then.

Eamon's brow furrowed and Rich looked amused. Around the group there was bafflement. Only Tanya was managing to look intrigued by Fergus' outlandish statement. *Well, well!* I thought, deciding that Tanya might have transferred her affections away from Rich in favour of Fergus.

I had no idea why.

"How so?" Eamon prompted.

"I don't see another logical explanation. This site is a well known hub of UFO activity. It's been shut off from the public for years... and I think we may have just discovered the reason why."

"You think aliens poisoned Christine and then stabbed her? Did this alien also dress up in some kind of glowing military uniform and run down the corridor?" Rich asked, sarcasm practically dripping from his voice.

"Glowing?" Fergus narrowed his eyes at me before continuing. "I will be investigating every possible angle, but I think it could be plausible. Aliens mostly come into contact with our military personnel, so this visitor from outer space might have worn the uniform as a disguise, hoping to blend in."

"But why kill Christine?" Eamon pressed, itching to say that this was all utter nonsense.

"That is an excellent question, and one I believe can be answered... with a bag search," Fergus finished, surprising everyone present - myself included.

"That's a sensible idea," I said, shooting Fergus a sideways look to see if it had been his plan all along. He studiously avoided making eye contact with me.

"What do you hope to find out about aliens from a bag search?" Rich asked, still looking amused.

"I think this visitor might have planted certain items in our cases." Fergus said it like he really believed it. Even I wasn't sure if this was part of his method to diffuse all of the tension with a ridiculous theory, or if he genuinely did think we'd been visited by E.T.

"A bag search! That's not a bad idea," Eamon trumpeted. "One of you lot is hiding something. We're all here. We should do it together and right this second, so no one can hide anything." He gave everyone the beady eye.

There were murmurs of consent. As one group, we went into Sylvia's room, apologised for invading her privacy, and then went through the small suitcase she'd brought with her. Everyone eyed the knitting bag. It was agreed that it would be removed from her room and placed in with Christine. Nothing that appeared to relate to the crime was found in Sylvia's luggage, but I hadn't really expected there to be anything. Whoever was actually responsible for the crime had already placed enough suspicion on the elderly lady.

The next room was Christine's. After a brief debate, we decided that we wouldn't go through her bags. It was doubtful that she'd be carrying something pertaining to her murder, and if she'd been killed for an item in her possession, it would surely have already been taken. That was the logic used to make the decision. The truth was, no one wanted to return to the room where the smell of death lingered. We dropped the bag in and shut the door again.

Instead, we went next door to Eamon. His luggage contained nothing incriminating either - something that he'd been adamant about from the start of this exercise.

Rich Strauss' bag inspection was the first to turn something up. His neat designer man bag was opened and the contents inspected. Neatly folded underwear and shirts stared back at us.

"See? Nothing groundbreaking apart from some fantastic boutique underwear from a little shop in London I would be happy to share with you," he drawled whilst Tanya dispassionately flipped the contents around. She really did seem to have lost the hots for Rich.

"Hey, wait!" I said, just before she was about to slam down the lid with some definite disappointment. I reached in and pulled out the sharpie marker pen I'd seen poking out from one of the rolled up pairs of boxer shorts.

"That's not mine," Rich said far too quickly.

"Let me guess... you have no idea how it got there?" Fergus stepped in, looking rather too pleased with himself. He turned to me with a questioning look on his face.

"It's impossible to know for sure, but it does look like it might be the pen that was used to write the message on the flower," I allowed.

Rich looked grave. "I'm sure you're right, but it's not mine. Someone must have planted it in there," he protested.

"Huh!" was all Eamon had to say to that.

Our group inspection continued with Duncan and Bella. Both of their suitcases looked well-travelled. I wondered how many competitions Bella had won before this unlucky trip and where they'd travelled. I knew that 'compers', as they were known, entered hundreds of competitions a day and often won experiences that even money couldn't buy. The interior of one of the bags revealed more interesting items. A kindle case monogrammed with B.R.H (empty due to the confiscation of all communication devices) a pair of remark-ably thick woollen socks, and some rather fancy silk boxers further fuelled my suspicion that Bella may have been on a winning streak. I knew it wasn't strictly fair to judge items against people - personal preferences could always surprise you - but Duncan and Bella didn't strike me as the frivolous sort.

Rich conducted the honours when we inspected Tanya's room. I wasn't sure what exactly had happened between the pair, but he was practically sneering whilst sorting through her clothes, underwear, and fluffy socks.

"Nothing there," Tanya concluded smugly when Rich was forced to admit defeat.

We briefly searched Lorna and Jack's bags without finding anything. I glanced at Rich and cleared my throat. "We found a set of master keys with both of your names on it in a bag with the fork. Do either of you know why they might have been there?"

Both guides paled.

Lorna turned accusingly to face Jack. "I knew I shouldn't have left them with you!"

"Hey! I already told you I hung them up as soon as we were released to our work station at lunchtime yesterday. I remember putting them on the hook," Jack protested, looking panicked by the implications the missing keys had for him.

"Well, they were gone last night!" Lorna muttered.

Everyone looked from one guide to the other, but there seemed to be nothing more to say. Jack or Lorna could have taken the bunch of keys and used them to commit murder, but they could also have been stolen by someone who'd seen an opportunity.

Next, we moved all the way back down the row of rooms to Lady Isabella's. Something about her well-spoken nature and the feeling I was sure we all had that she was used to moving in the upper circles of society made everyone apologetic. To her credit, Lady Isabella accepted the whole thing with excellent grace. In the end, Sylvia was the one who conducted her bag search. She was about to shut it again when Fergus stepped forwards and peeled a long glove off where it had stuck on the top of her suitcase. We all stared at the red smear it left behind.

"It **is** my glove," Lady Isabella confirmed. "But I have no idea at all as to how that nasty stain got on it. I haven't worn that pair since being here. They're rather old and worn out."

I shook my head, feeling this mystery sink further into the mire of doubt.

"One more room! We'd better hurry. There's only ten minutes before the next challenge begins and I haven't had my fill of sandwiches yet," Eamon announced, his hunger overcoming his standoffish attitude.

We dutifully trooped into the room Fergus and I were sharing and the search began. I discovered I wasn't at all surprised when a whole pack of chai teabags turned up inside my suitcase. Someone really was playing us all and in such a way that made our suspicions plausible. I'd identified the poison, so wasn't it probable that I could have been the one to use it?

Fergus' suitcase was cracked open next. Everyone stared at the military uniform lying on top of his clothes.

"Oh, come on! That would never fit me," Fergus said, picking it up and demonstrating that the wearer had been considerably shorter and narrower than he was.

"You might have bought it deliberately small for this very moment," Rich suggested. "It was dark when you were spotted wearing it."

"I never wore it! I've never seen it before in my life," Fergus protested, looking amused by all of the fuss.

"You did suggest that aliens would have chosen military wear if they were invading us, or something," Bella meekly suggested, before blushing under scrutiny.

"That's because I genuinely believe they might imper-sonate military personnel. I didn't say anything about personally impersonating..." he shook his head, tripping over his own words. "It's clearly not mine. For one, I'd have sourced the genuine article. This is just a tacky costume." He pointed out the wobbly stitching and cheap polyester accents. "Someone is clearly messing with us," he finished, voicing my own thoughts out loud.

"Then it's someone who looks innocent who is actually the killer," Eamon said, squinting round the circle and conveniently forgetting that his case hadn't been tampered with.

"Not necessarily. The killer could have framed themselves to play the victim and appear less guilty," I said, wanting to play devil's advocate.

"We...uh...need to start the next challenge. You know bad things happen when we're late," Jack prompted when the silence had gone on too long.

We trooped back into the dining hall. I grabbed as many of the remaining sandwiches as I could. Rich kept that same amused look on his face when he selected a couple himself. I decided there and then that I wasn't going to pay any attention to what the South African thought or did.

Especially now that the pen had been found in his luggage.

I chewed on a smoked salmon sandwich whilst I thought about that. The other additions to peoples' luggage had been obvious - farcical, even, in the case of the blood-stained glove stuck to the top of Lady Isabella's suitcase. But the pen was subtle - just like the writing on the flower had been. Plus, Rich Strauss had the most obvious connection to Christine Montague and the most obvious motive for murder. He'd been working with her, and his boss certainly hadn't been a saint. There could be any number of reasons for Rich to snap.

As we walked across the hall towards the room indicated by our guides, I couldn't help but wonder if we'd already found Christine's killer. And we still had to spend one more night alone together. Did I really want to get any closer to the truth?

Whilst the others rushed towards the door of the next

challenge, eager to avoid a repeat of this morning's dramatic motivator, I hesitated, feeling the book inside the overalls I'd reclaimed from Fergus. With no one else around, I pulled it out and flipped through *The Language of Flowers* until I arrived at the entry for snapdragon, which revealed its victorian hidden meaning. A single word jumped out at me.

Deception

8

CLOSE ENCOUNTERS OF THE SEVENTH KIND

"I declare that this challenge is impossible!" a red and sweaty-faced Eamon announced half an hour into our first task of the afternoon. I hated to quit on anything in life - I now understood that it was the main reason I had dedicated so long to both chemistry and my old relationship - but in this instance, I was starting to lean toward's Eamon's view.

The challenge had seemed fairly simple at first glance. It was a virtual challenge in which you had to place the flowers displayed on the screen in vases that corresponded with the month of the year they were most commonly available. The problem was, some flowers had a flowering span of several months, some of them even had a second flush, and there was quite a lot of debate over which months which plants and flowers were available. The challenge would only be finished when everything was in the place it should be. The course designer had known what a fiend they were being and had included percentages below the months that told us how close the displays were to being correct, but that didn't always help. To make matters even worse, we'd been given ten lives… and we'd already lost three of them.

"What happens when we run out of lives? How bad do you think it will be?" Bella fretted, tugging on her dishevelled ponytail. Everyone's appearance had suffered somewhat from the terrible start to the morning and then the stress of the following challenges.

"Who knows?" Rich said with a casual shrug. "I didn't even want to be here," he added in a lower tone.

I silently raised my eyes to the heavens. This course did rely quite heavily on the shared knowledge of those taking it and their willingness to work as a team. It was strange, but I did think that I was picking up a few tips. Were it not for the murder, it might even have been fun. However, the ambiguity of the punishments for when we got things wrong were starting to get on my nerves. Worrying about an unknown meant that everyone was overcautious in their choices, and whenever someone got something wrong, there was definitely a feeling of the group blaming them.

I also suspected that the course designer had taken into account each and every person who was attending - as the earlier poison challenge had demonstrated - and was relying on them sharing their skills with others. What the designer hadn't accounted for was that we would be losing one of our number - and the one we'd lost might have known more about seasonal flowers than the rest of us put together. Christine had excelled at designing gardens throughout the year. Gardens that had to look their best at very specific times of the year. While she might not be an expert flower arranger, she would certainly have known which flowers cropped up at which point during the calendar.

Rich came and stood next to me, running a hand through his messily styled hair. "Too bad we can't hack the system and get ourselves out of here, right?"

"I'm sure we'll get it correct in the end. The punishment is probably only something like another glitter bomb," I diplomatically suggested, unsure where Rich wanted this conversation to go. Fergus and Eamon were still looking sparkly. I privately thought it worked for Fergus but not for crusty old Eamon.

"Or it could be something much worse. Remember the shortbread?" Rich pointed out, rather annoyingly.

I tried to make light of it. "It would only have been bad if we'd actually eaten it. The course designer never expected us to."

"They never expected a bunch of people to be locked in with a murderer either, but here we are."

I did my best to keep my expression blank. If someone had asked me to put money on who was likeliest to have killed Christine, the person who made the most sense was the man standing right next to me. I wondered if he was really oblivious to the fact, or if this was all part of his game.

"I wish Christine was here," Rich said, surprising me. "She was really good when it came to figuring out creative ways to break the rules. Sure, she didn't exactly make any friends on her way up to the top, but she could always outmanoeuvre the competition." He grinned. "She was tolerating all of this stuff during the first day, but if she'd been here today I guarantee she'd probably have found a way to melt the lock on the door, or something crazy like that." There was a note of admiration in his voice that made me uncertain all over again about Rich being the killer. Could you admire someone but still want them dead?

"Who gets control of Christine's company now that she's gone?" I asked on a whim.

Rich shot me a look of amusement, triggered by my careless statement. "The bank and Her Majesty's government, I assume. The business has been turning a profit recently, but starting a business like that from scratch doesn't come cheap. Christine had a lot of debts. Now she's gone, it'll be time to pay up." He shot me a thoughtful look. "You grow flowers… why don't you tell me more about your business?"

Now it was my turn to shoot him a look that said he was hardly being subtle in his inquiries. "I'm definitely not in the kind of league Christine was. Nor do I ever really want to be," I hastily added, knowing that Rich would probably suggest I did my best to rise up to get there.

He smiled a little ruefully. "Shame. I've been watching you through all of these challenges. You really know your stuff and you're sensible - not hotheaded. If I've learned anything it's that being hotheaded gets you nowhere in business. You might know more than the guy you're up against, but if you lose your cool, the man who uses his head, and not his passion, will always win and know when the time is right to strike." He made a fist with his hand and his eyes flashed cold steel before the smile returned to his expression. "I understand that you don't want to turn into someone like Christine, but I think you're still ambitious. I can see it in everything you do. You want to achieve… and I think I could help you to do it." He reached out and rested a hand on my arm for a moment. I looked at the hand and he took it away again.

"Thank you for the offer. I'm pretty sure I can't afford your services, but I'll consider it," I said, just to be polite.

"Oh, I would work pro-bono in your case," he promised.

I raised my eyebrows. "Surely someone with your work experience would be able to walk into an excellent job now that I assume you're looking for new employment."

"Don't be so sure. Being the number one suspect when it comes to your boss' unsolved murder is hardly a selling point. Tell me I'm wrong?"

I felt my cheeks warm for a second. But it was the only semi-logical theory I currently had.

"Anyway, maybe I'm done with working that kind of job. High stakes business takes it out of you. Perhaps I just want to settle down in the English countryside with a flower grower who doesn't want her business to grow too big." He looked thoughtfully at me.

I felt my stomach twist into all kinds of knots and turned away to try to regain some sense of clarity. My eyes found Fergus across the room. He was watching me with a bemused look on his face. He silently raised his eyebrows at me. I diverted my gaze from him, too. Honestly, I had no idea what either man thought they were playing at.

"I think we should all be focusing on the challenge at hand. It's hardly pragmatic to be standing around talking about the future when we don't know how to get out of here, or what happens if we don't complete everything in time," I said, hoping to end the conversation.

Something cleared in Rich's expression. "Right you are! We should seize the moment rather than wallowing in indecision." I watched with mounting concern as he walked over to the touch screen and moved several of the flowers around. Alarms blared when he got two out of three incorrect and we lost further lives. Within moments, the group had surrounded Rich and pulled him back from the touchscreen. "I was just moving things along! We're never going to get out of here unless someone puts it all on the line. We've got to take a risk!"

"The man has a point," Fergus spoke up from his place in the corner, surprising everyone by agreeing with Rich. "However, he's not the one to take the risk. We need to elect someone who will make the final decisions, and then we let them get on with it. We're getting nowhere debating these final flower choices. We could end up spending the night in here if we aren't careful. I'm voting for Diana." He looked towards me with trust in his dark eyes.

"Thanks a bunch," I muttered under my breath, knowing that Fergus' idea came with the dubious honour of being the mug who was probably first in line to receive whatever punishment there'd be for getting the choices wrong.

But he wasn't the only one thinking along those lines.

"I vote for Diana, too," Eamon said, raising his right hand which still showed traces of blue glitter.

"Me too," Rich said from where he'd been restrained, not wanting to be left out of this ridiculous vote that Fergus had initiated.

"I think that would be a good idea. Out of all of us, you do have the most hands-on seasonal flower knowledge," Sylvia said, smiling encouragingly at me. The others murmured their assent.

I looked around, hoping for someone else to step forwards but no one did. I was the sacrificial lamb. "I'm really not that experienced..." I muttered, stepping towards the screen with dread in the pit of my stomach. Whatever forfeit I'd face if all the lives were lost, I was sure it would be something worse than a glitter explosion. That had been this morning's challenge when the day had been starting on a lighter note (murder aside). There was something about this task that felt like the consequences of failure would be much worse.

I took a deep breath and studied the flowers in front of me. The ones I'd been sure of had already been sorted when I'd staked my reputation on their placements. Now I was left with a whole bunch of maybes.

I got the first three right.

The fourth one got the buzzer and another life vanished. The fifth one followed. We were down six lives with four remaining. I tried some more combinations, and got a few right, but two more lives went down the hatch. I had two more chances before my luck ran out.

I felt a drop of sweat drip down the back of my neck as I sensed all eyes watching me, willing me to get it right. I moved the worryingly generic 'ornamental grasses' into October's bouquet and breathed a sigh of relief when the progress bar showed 100% for that particular arrangement. I was left with two bouquets - March and December, that needed finishing and a whole raft of options. Some of them were false friends. I knew that a lot of the fancier orchids were imported and never grown in the UK without copious greenhouse help and manipulation. Anything that needed to be forced or coddled was not in the running on this challenge. The flower arranging we were learning was definitely geared towards what our native country could produce - something which I approved of when it came to sustainability and good business morals.

I took a deep breath and sorted them the best way I could using logic and guesswork. The buzzer sounded on the first, and I quickly moved the second, knowing it could result in disaster. March's bouquet was complete. With that small jolt of success under my belt, I made the final selection, praying that I was right and mahonia x media was a December option.

The sound of the fanfare nearly made me fall over in shock when my ears wrongly interpreted it as the buzzer. The door clicked open and the group cheered and patted me on the back. Whilst everyone filed through into whatever lay beyond the door, I hung back by the screen, feeling my heart rate return to normal.

"Good thing you got it right. It probably wouldn't have been too dramatic, but before I was dragged away, I spotted wires that look like they might have belonged to some kind of flash and bang device," Rich said conversationally.

"Flash and bang?" I asked, looking skeptically to where he was pointing.

"I also used to mess around with pyrotechnics in my misspent youth," he said with an easy shrug. "Growing up in Cape Town, it paid to be handy with all kinds of things. Mostly people live sheltered lives in compounds out there, but with the crime and employment rate not exactly brilliant, it paid to have some extra skills to hand."

I silently observed that when he said 'pyrotechnics' he wasn't talking about the kind you saw on stage at a music festival. Rich was an enigma and not one I was certain I wanted to unwrap.

I indicated that we should probably follow the others into the second room. For just a moment, Rich seemed to want to hang back and even took a step closer to me. When Fergus stuck his head back through the door and told us to get a move on as the next challenge couldn't start until the door shut I felt a flutter of relief. Rich was certainly focusing a lot of his attention on me. While I could appreciate that he was an attractive man, and a far cry from boring, the situation hardly leant itself to us building any kind of trust. In any case, I was happy with my current situation and didn't want to have a man potentially interested in anything more than friendship.

I willingly walked past Fergus and flashed him a grateful smile. Across the room, Tanya scowled at me, but I ignored it. We had a challenge to focus on. Whatever else was bouncing around was simply not a concern.

Not unless it led to a second murder anyway.

The door clicked shut behind us and the lights went out.

Plunged into blackness there was panic as people moved and others shouted at everyone to stay still. I felt a stab of fear that the darkness was dangerous. If a killer did walk among our ranks, no one wanted to be alone in the dark with them. And what if this whole thing was a set-up, as some had suggested? Even with these doubts running through my head, I kept my cool and backed up, so that I had the solid surface of the wall behind me. Fewer people would run into me, and if anyone was sneaking around, they'd have a hard time getting behind me.

"I think I've had enough surprises for a lifetime. How about you?" Rich's accented drawl came just a few centimetres away from my ear. I wondered how he'd found me in the darkness and came to the conclusion that he'd sought the wall the same as I had. I felt the vibration of someone joining us on my other side.

"Our money is totally on Rich being the killer, isn't it?" Fergus whispered in my other ear.

"He's right next to me!" I hissed back, knowing that the South African would have to be deaf as a post to have not overheard Fergus' accusation. So much for any remaining subtlety as to where suspicions currently lay.

I made a silly 'ooph' sound when someone ran into me and the air exited my lungs.

"Sorry! Fergus? Is that you? I hate this. It's really scary. Do you mind if I just stand here next to you?" Tanya's voice came from the inky blackness.

"Not Fergus," I managed, utterly bemused by the fake 'little girl' voice Tanya was using.

"I think he's over the other side of the room," Fergus said in a passable impression of Eamon's voice.

"Oh, right. Thanks," Tanya said. We all heard her tripping off as she tried to travel through the blackness searching for Fergus.

"So... this is awkward," Rich said, breaking the silence that had descended amongst we three wall dwellers. "I know you guys aren't going to believe me, but I really didn't kill her. It's like I told you already... Christine had enemies. I'm not saying she deserved to die, but I am saying that she probably gave plenty of people plenty of reasons to want her out of the game."

"Plenty of people is not specific enough, Rich!" I countered. "That kind of motive would mean it is someone who knows her... someone here who is covering up the truth. The only person who seems to have any connection whatsoever with Christine is you."

"Don't be so dense. I'm the obvious choice! I'm probably the exact reason that whoever it is picked this moment to kill Christine. I'm the one being framed."

"I don't think that's true," Fergus countered from my other side. "It seems to me like everyone is being framed... and I think you were hoping to push suspicion that way to keep any from landing on you. But you forgot the pen. We weren't supposed to find the writing on the snapdragon."

"Don't be so sure. If everything else is a setup, why not the flower and the pen, too?" Rich pushed back.

"Fergus! I knew you were over here. What do you think's going to happen to us?" Tanya simpered, having clearly overheard the conversation. I wondered how everyone else was faring in the dark.

"We'll either be stuck in the dark until someone fixes the power cut, or the lights will come back on," Fergus said with a complete absence of humour.

"You're so smart," Tanya told him.

Fergus cleared his throat. "Actually, I think I can see something now. It's glowing, look..." I could only assume he was pointing, but seeing as none of us could see a thing, I looked in all directions before I noticed it, too. Somewhere off to the left, there was a definite glow... and it was getting bigger.

"Is that... fire?!" Rich said, sounding just as alarmed as I felt.

All at once, the glow grew brighter and speakers blared to life.

"Happy Birthday to you, Happy Birthday to you, Happy Birthday dear Diana, Happy Birthday to you!" an unseen chorus sung. In the next instant the glow was gone and the screen lit up, allowing us to now see that the fire had been on the screen all along and was in fact merely candles on a chocolate cake, held by our virtual teacher, Damien.

He smiled and placed the cake down. "Now, this is a last minute addition, but we heard it was somebody's birthday today."

In the dim light of the screen everyone turned to look at me. I shook myself and remembered that he was right. In all of the drama, I'd forgotten about it.

"As you have a birthday, we have a birthday challenge for you." The lights rose up as he spoke and revealed flowers in pails. There were also various adornments including ribbons, bows, stickers, ornamental bugs on sticks and other interesting items that were all clearly supposed to be used in this challenge. There were even a few pots of glitter that I hoped no one would think about using after this morning's glitter attack. It was the bane of florists for a good reason. I privately thought that the adage of the customer always being right should never apply when it came to glitter requests.

"As you already know, a florist is required to create flowers for all occasions. They must also know what the client likes. Diana… you will be excluded from this challenge beyond the initial questioning and you will only answer the questions asked and not provide any further help. Diana's floral preferences have been logged into the system ahead of time. You may ask her three questions to establish what she may or may not prefer in a bouquet before she will leave the room and you will get to work. I will judge when you have completed the challenge.

I looked wildly around. No one had asked me any questions about anything! What was this simulation talking about? How could it possibly know my preferences? I glanced at Fergus, who was studiously avoiding making eye contact. *Oh.* Well that could change a few things. I shot him a look that said 'I can't believe you!'. How was anyone going to pass this challenge when Fergus was the one who'd clearly supplied the answers?

"I guess we should start!" Eamon announced, stepping forwards. "Let's start with something simple, shall we? What are your favourite colours?"

Good question, I silently thought and looked towards the back of the room where Fergus was mouthing something at me. "Yellow…een," I said when Fergus shook his head frantically. "Green," I corrected, receiving mystified looks from the group. "Purple and… brown?!" I finished, incredulous. Those were the worst colour choices I'd ever heard.

Most of my listeners looked dismayed, but Rich was already starting to laugh at my ridiculous choices.

"What sort of decorations do you like?" Lady Isabella said, looking hopeful that this was an area that might give us some clues.

Fergus was miming something by flinging his hands around wildly. "Big bows? Lots of frills?" He shrugged, apparently that was close enough.

"Lovely," Lady Isabella said, her tone telling me that she thought the opposite. "Anything else?"

I raised my eyebrows at Fergus who nodded and pointed at the most atrocious pot of fake fairies on sticks. "Fairies. Love them," I said, any good humour almost completely vanished. The group was so focused on getting this challenge right no one seemed to have noticed I was being led by a complete moron at the back of the room. Only Rich looked amused to the point of laughter by my ludicrously out of character choices.

Fergus shook his sleeve and pointed at the shower that fell to the floor. I sighed out loud. "And glitter. I absolutely adore glitter," I finished, hating the words that passed between my lips.

There were groans all round. I hung my head in a silent apology. I would get Fergus back for this one way or another. It just added to my suspicions that Fergus wasn't what you'd call thoughtful. I knew I was always going to look at anything suggested by him with a healthy dollop of suspicion from now on.

"What kind of container do you tend to go for?" Sylvia asked, arching her eyebrows behind her glasses. Somehow I sensed this was going to be the final nail in the coffin in terms of any remaining shreds of good taste the group may have once believed I had. It was a good thing I wasn't trying to sell flowers to any of them.

I looked hopefully in Fergus' direction, praying that he'd redeem himself with this choice. He pointed towards the corner of the room. I followed his finger.

I shut my eyes and then opened them again. "I can't get enough of those horrifically kitsch glitter-twig things over there," I informed them, nodding towards the pots Fergus had chosen for me.

He crossed his arms and pouted. Apparently my level of effort wasn't high enough for his liking. He'd just have to deal with it. His bad choices could have been the ruination of everyone, if I'd been honest about my preferences.

"The questions are complete. With your new knowledge, you will craft your birthday bouquets. Diana, please step through the door," the man on the screen said, smiling as if I hadn't just spouted the most ridiculous list of preferences ever. I supposed in a way it was perfect. People did make some horrible choices when it came to what they liked, but in the end, it was your job to give them what they wanted - no matter how poor their taste was.

You just probably shouldn't ever post it on social media... or admit it was your own work.

I shot Fergus one last scathing look and then walked through the doorway. It shut behind me and I was left alone in an empty room with my thoughts.

I was still thinking everything over and feeling that there was something I was missing when the door opened again and Fergus practically jumped through.

"What happened?" I asked, confused as to why he was the only one who'd finished.

"It's an 'everyone for themselves' type of challenge. I was hoping it might be. I did my arrangement, got it judged without anyone seeing it, and got through."

"You preplanned it?" I knew I was frowning, wondering if there was anything else Fergus had preplanned... like a murder. Although I couldn't see a single reason why he'd have wanted Christine Montague dead. He hadn't even known about her before this trip, and I genuinely believed that. Watching Fergus on this course over the past couple of days had reinforced my feeling that he was not remotely interested in anything horticultural. The only growing things he cared about were plants caused by strange soil or crop circles.

"I didn't know anything was going to happen. To be honest, when I gave the guy who called up your preferences for a challenge I was supposed to keep secret, I was as honest as I could be about what you liked. He thought I already had it written down because we're so close and all that."

I nodded and then frowned. "Wait. You honestly think I love glitter and bows and... brown flowers?!" I wasn't sure which one was the most offensive.

"Of course not. That's why I'm through and the others aren't. I told them pretty much the exact opposite of what you liked. To be honest, I just thought it would be fun to be the first to win a challenge for once, but when the door opened for me I walked right on through and it shut behind me." He shrugged. "It's kind of useful when you think about it. We've got some time to talk about the mystery we're bang splat in the middle of right now."

"Won't the others be through in a few seconds?" I asked.

Fergus shrugged again not meeting my gaze. "My final arrangement may have landed on the floor on my way out. I'm sure they'll piece it together and figure out the truth, but I reckon it will take at least ten minutes before anyone else gets through that door. Plenty of time to conspire and eat cake."

I looked at the table and discovered that Fergus was right about the cake. His entry into the room must have triggered some hidden mechanism that had allowed a sticky chocolate cake with candles burning on top to rise up from where it had been concealed.

"Are you gonna blow them out, or am I going to have to cut around them?" Fergus asked.

I blew air across the candles, using it in lieu of a sigh. I sighed a lot when I was around Fergus.

"What if it's poisoned?" I asked (halfheartedly).

Fergus looked at the cake and then back at me. "Is it?"

"Probably not," I concluded. Unless someone had managed to tamper with it - the same way someone had interfered with Christine's tea - then I didn't see why the cake would be poisoned. We'd already been thrown that curve ball. I believed this genuinely was a birthday cake that everyone was supposed to share with me. I reflected that, unless the group got their act together and figured out that they'd been fed some false information, there wasn't going to be a lot of cake left by the time they arrived.

I wasn't sure there was going to be a lot of Fergus or myself left either when they did make it through.

"So... who killed her then?" Fergus asked me in-between mouthfuls of chocolate cake.

"How should I know?" I batted back, silently debating and then deciding to have some cake myself. I had basically missed lunch after all.

"You're a scientist. You're good at working things out. You see things that other people miss. Who else is better placed to get to the bottom of the mystery? Plus, you've been asking all of the right questions. You must have something figured out by now."

I opened my mouth and shut it again. "I was just trying to see why someone might want Christine Montague out of the way. It was curiosity, not any big investigation. That should be left to the police."

Fergus rolled his eyes and swallowed his mouthful of cake. "You keep saying things like that, but at the same time, you're asking questions about Elliot Harving and joining the dots together. You're Sherlock and I'm your Watson, the cheerful companion, whose quirky characteristics and unpredictable actions are what really causes the mystery to be solved - only they allow the credit to be taken by their intelligent, but egotistical, friend."

"I don't think that's how those stories go..."

Fergus waved a silencing hand. "The point is, I bet you know the answer. You might not realise it, but it's probably there, staring you in the face."

I looked hopelessly around the room but the only thing staring me in the face was Fergus... and the knowledge that I'd just eaten far too much chocolate cake. "You said there was a conspiracy theory about the Harving incident?" I said, hoping to distract him from his crazy idea that I'd somehow got it all figured out.

"Yes - that it was deliberate sabotage or deliberate negligence. To be honest, it started out as a theory but was later proven - which was why the sculptors were convicted." He waggled his eyebrows at me. "See... some of my theories do turn out to be correct all along. I'm not a crackpot."

"But was it ever explained why the sculptors would have wanted to sabotage their own work? Did they mean for people to get hurt?" I pressed, wondering if a motive had ever been established.

A line appeared between Fergus' brows. "I don't think they ever confessed to the crime or explained why they did it. They just ended up in prison."

"And later died in there," I filled in, shaking my head. "You know what? Rich said something in the first challenge we did today. He said Christine had a way of getting what she wanted and breaking the rules to get it. What if she's the one who wanted Elliot Harving out of the way and she's the one who sabotaged the sculpture?" It was the most plausible theory so far.

"That makes sense. It's all about Elliot Harving. I'm guessing it wouldn't be a stretch for someone to believe that Christine was involved in his demise. Although... I'm not sure why." I thought about it. "Probably jealousy. Elliot was an up and coming garden designer. Perhaps Christine didn't want to risk the competition."

Fergus frowned in-between mouthfuls of cake. "Killing him seems a bit extreme when you can just discredit the man."

"She might not have known that he would die. How would she have known when...?" I stopped talking as several things came together for me. Half-remembered words and comments made sense, and I knew I was on the edge of finding out the truth and the killer responsible for the murder of Christine Montague.

"What kind of trick was that? I thought this course was about building teamwork," Rich said when he walked through the door. All talk and thoughts about murder would have to wait. After my sudden flash of inspiration the only person I genuinely believed I could trust was Fergus. I wasn't sure which of the other course members was the one feeding the rest of us a line.

"I had nothing to do with it," I said, throwing Fergus to the wolves.

He glared at me with chocolate smeared around his mouth. I smiled sweetly in return. This was a battle he'd have to fight on his own.

"You seem to have figured it out just fine," Fergus pointed out.

Rich shrugged self-deprecatingly. "I wasn't convinced by your answers from the start. I knew that a woman like Diana wouldn't have that kind of taste." He looked at me.

It was as if the whole room disappeared and it was just us, alone and looking deep into each others' souls.

I blinked to get rid of *that* unsettling feeling.

"I dunno... the glitter is growing on me," I said to try to divert the mood.

"It's growing on everyone. It's gained a consciousness of its own," Fergus added, not helping anything.

Rich shook his head and gave me a look that said oh so clearly 'why do you hang out with this idiot?'. I looked away, not trusting myself to make a good decision on how to look in response.

Tanya was the next one to arrive and she looked even less pleased than Rich.

"What's the big idea?"

"It wasn't anything to do with me," I said whilst Fergus threw his hands up in the air and looked betrayed.

"I thought it would be funny. Something to lighten the mood, you know?" Fergus said, addressing Tanya.

The change to her expression was remarkable. She beamed so brightly it was as if the sun had suddenly broken through the clouds. "I should have known. You have such a great sense of humour! It's just what we all needed."

"I know," Fergus said without any trace of shame whatsoever. "Chocolate cake? There won't be any left soon."

"Oo no! I don't really like cake," Tanya announced. And just like that, I dismissed all chances of anything ever working out between her and Fergus.

The final challenge was rather predictable. It meshed all of the skills we'd learned that day together. We were in a greenhouse area and told to forage but only for plants that were in season for the month we were in right now. Any incorrect choices would result in penalties. Everyone looked to Fergus when the word 'penalty' was mentioned and, as predicted, Fergus was the first one to make a critical error. When he presented his 'final product', with all the swagger of a student who finished their homework five minutes before the lesson began, there was a small explosion as a hammer smashed down on his arrangement.

Fergus shrugged. That punishment wasn't such a big deal. No problem. He would make another. Before he could walk away from the judging platform water showered down on top of him followed by a whole bucket of glitter. "I think someone is running out of ideas," Fergus commented, inspecting his multi-coloured shine. The final icing on the cake was when the icing on the cake hit him in the face. A birthday cake the same as the one we'd eaten earlier struck a direct hit.

Fergus spat glitter and icing out of his mouth, pulling a bemused face. "The challenge is a combination of everything we learned today. I guess the punishment is, too," he concluded, a lot less smug than he had been.

"Couldn't have happened to a better person," I said before primly returning to my own arrangement which I noted was nearly finished. I felt that I still lacked some of the finesse and skills that some florists I'd admired over the years possessed but my knowledge of floriculture and when things were in season had done me proud and I was hopeful that this was a challenge I was going to ace.

I placed my finished arrangement of chrysanthemums and rose-hips on the judgement table and waited, wondering for a second if I was going to be covered in glitter and cake.

Emilia beamed on screen and I was congratulated on my success. It would appear that the team spirit nature of the course was diminishing, as I was instructed to leave the greenhouse and enjoy the dinner that had just been automatically cooked for us all. I was certain that things like automatic dinner were supposed to be part of the course's selling points, but, in all honesty, I couldn't wait for tomorrow to be finished and to be able to make a return to the real world beyond the walls of the bunker.

Dinner was fish and chips cooked in some healthy, equally trendy, manner - that in my mind completely ruined the concept. I sat alone in the dining hall and picked at my food, wondering who would be next to walk through the door.

I was immensely surprised to find it was Fergus.

"Before you ask how I cheated, I want you to know that I didn't cheat at all," he informed me, sitting down behind a plate and digging in. I was starting to get the impression that

Fergus didn't mind so much what he was eating so long as there was something to eat.

"Then what did you do?" I asked, knowing there had to be some kind of trickery involved.

Fergus made a big show of looking offended. "I can learn things, you know! I'm good at learning, and this course has taught me a lot."

I raised my eyebrows at him. While what he'd just said was plausible, it didn't fit with my idea of Fergus and his non-conformity to traditional methods when faced with just about anything.

He grinned and I knew I was right. "I watched you make your arrangement and then copied it pretty much flower for flower. I have no pride in my own work, so I borrowed yours."

"I should have guessed," I said, considering it. "I suppose that isn't unreasonable. Unsporting, but not unreasonable."

"Thank you!" Fergus acted like I'd just paid him a great compliment.

I shook my head and decided to eat something.

"So... alone again at last," Fergus said, grinning at me over his dinner plate.

"I haven't solved any mysteries," I informed him, spearing something that I assumed was supposed to pass as a chip.

"Have you solved the mystery of your suitor, Rich?" Fergus asked, making me choke on the mouthful I'd just taken.

"Suitor? Are we living in medieval England?"

"He's been following you around like a puppy all day."

I pushed my auburn hair back from my forehead. "You really think so?" Of course I'd noticed the attentions of the South African. He'd been nothing if not persistent, but I wasn't interested in any kind of relationship. It had been a long time since my last one had ended, but I was still licking my wounds and was unwilling to open up fresh ones.

But that didn't mean I wasn't above pulling Fergus' leg a little.

"It is rather surprising, isn't it?" Fergus acknowledged with seriousness that made me want to hit him.

"Is it? I'm young, in my prime, I own a business, I possess a sparkling wit and intelligence..." I countered.

"Young-ish." Fergus knocked back.

I glared at him. I was not willing to kiss goodbye to my youth just yet - no matter what my birthday might say. "No need to be jealous, Fergus. Tanya seems very interested in you and your work."

"No jealousy here. I just have an interest in your happiness and wellbeing. I don't think it's a good idea for you to shack up with the most obvious murder suspect."

"Tanya's hardly above suspicion! She knew who Christine was before this course. She claimed she even knocked on Christine's door the night before she died in order to tell her how much of a fan she was, but she might have played that part in order to protect herself from any suspicion when her rival turned up dead with puncture wounds in her back. "

"Tanya is just attracted to success and a man who knows what being a man is all about. Didn't you see the way she switched her attentions to me when she discovered the truth? She'd heard of me, too, remember?"

I frowned, recalling that piece of information. It had struck me as strange at the time. Could it have anything to do with the murder that was currently baffling us all?

"It's not that implausible! In the right circles I'm quite well known," Fergus said, interpreting my frown as a slight against him.

"No doubt," I said placatingly as I started on the fish and the rest of the group filed into the room.

"Only another 24 hours and we can all get out of here," Jack announced, probably breaking guide protocol by making it clear that it would be a relief to leave this exclusive course. I was betting he wouldn't be invited back if the course was repeated. I doubted that it would be. Murder was hardly a good advertisement - not when it came to flower arranging anyway.

I pushed the food around my plate again, my thoughts elsewhere. I didn't even react when Rich slid into the chair next to me and oh so causally bumped his leg against mine. But I couldn't ignore it when he reached out and touched my hand.

"Rich," I said, turning to him and speaking in as low a voice as I could manage. "Now really isn't the time. I'm sorry. You seem like a..." I'd been about to say nice but nice didn't really cover Rich. It was too plain to be applied to him. "...an interesting man," I finished, a little limply.

"Don't tell me I'm not your type?" Rich said, looking amused. The flashy-looking South African had probably never been told he wasn't someone's type.

"I'm not looking for anyone to date. I'm currently enjoying my own company," I said and then winced at how that sounded. "I'm focusing on my business."

"Plenty of people date whilst also focusing on their businesses. I already suggested that we work together," Rich said, pressing the issue.

I looked into his attractive face and saw Fergus' scowl out of the corner of my eye. "And I appreciate the offer. I'm just not looking for a partner at the moment."

Rich kept watching me without backing off. "So, what happened? Some guy put you off men, or something?"

Did I blink? I wasn't sure. "Nothing should have to have 'happened' in order for me to not be interested in having a relationship. Plenty of people are happy on their own!" Was I really having to defend my decision?

Rich gave me a disbelieving look. "Sure, but something did happen, right? Whatever it was, I'm not like that guy." He moved closer again.

I pushed my chair back. "Actually, I have a feeling you are. Exactly like that guy," I told him, seeing it for the first time. I pushed my chair back and stood up trying to ignore the smug expression on Fergus' face. "Excuse me, I think I'll get an early night," I said and walked off to sit in my shared room. With a bit of luck, Fergus would have brought along some books to read. Even literature based on little to no evidence and wild speculation was more inviting than being pushed into something I didn't want to do by Rich.

Ten minutes later, there was a knock on the door. "Who is it?"

"Me," Fergus said, opening it and coming in. He looked at the *Close Encounters of the Seventh Kind* book I was holding with some surprise.

"There was nothing else to read. And I wanted to know what 'the Seventh Kind' referred to. I thought there were only five kinds…" I told him.

"You're quite far into it."

"It's gripping… if you treat it like fiction," I said defensively. The book was supposed to be a firsthand account of one man's experience chasing after flying saucers, or whatever it was he liked to refer to them as, but it read like a trashy thriller, and sometimes a trashy thriller was just what the doctor ordered.

"It's a little out there even for me," Fergus confided, sitting down on his bed. "I prefer theoretical arguments which are more earth based. Even investigating this bunker was more of a whim than something I'm an expert in. Still…

it will make an interesting magazine article. I'll make a few quid from selling it to all the usual places."

"Is that how you make money?" I asked. Normally it would be considered rude to enquire about one's means of income, but Fergus was such an enigma about everything.

He waved a hand. "A lady never tells."

I shook my head and rolled over with the book. Typical Fergus - never giving a straight answer.

"You know… Tanya came over right after you ditched Rich so dramatically."

"Really? Which of you did she come over to?" I asked drily.

"I'll have you know that I have a lot going for me! She came over to me," Fergus clarified anyway. "She, uh, actually asked me if I wanted to change rooms - seeing as you might be upset over things not working out between you and Rich."

I pulled a face into the book. Had it been that obvious? I'd been trying to keep it subtle so Rich wasn't publicly humiliated, but if Tanya had noticed, I might have missed the mark. It wasn't entirely my fault. Rich shouldn't have pushed matters so hard. "Am I to conclude that, as you are still here, you didn't take her up on her offer?"

"That would probably be accurate, yes," Fergus said, sounding faintly amused by the whole thing. "I won't tell you what she said next."

I glared at the book and then sat up. "What did she say next?" I asked, as I was certain I was supposed to.

Fergus inspected his fingernails. "Something along the lines of us messing everyone around when we are so clearly vying for the other's attention."

"Vying for your attention? That's absolutely ridiculous!"

Fergus grinned at me. "Actually, she didn't say anything like that. I just thought it would be hilarious to see your reaction."

I threw the book at him.

When I opened my eyes and discovered the glowing hands on the alarm clock were pointing to 2:10 a.m., I was less than impressed. My first conscious thought was that the shenanigans of last night had better not be repeated. Just when I was concluding that my own jumpiness had caused me to spring awake something moved outside the room.

Someone was sneaking around at the dead of night.

9

RUNNING FROM MURDER

I threw on a jumper and my trainers, walking to the door and listening intently for a moment. I could hear the sounds of Fergus snoring from his bed so didn't bother trying to wake him up. That man could sleep through a tornado.

After holding my breath, I thought I could just make out the sounds of someone's footsteps disappearing along the corridor. With the memory of the figure dressed in the military costume at the forefront of my mind and the spectre of a murderer running loose in the bunker, I stepped out of the room and silently shut the door behind me. It was only when I was standing out in the silence of the empty corridor that I reflected I probably should have brought some kind of weapon along with me for company. I wanted to reassure myself that no one here had a motive to murder me, but I wasn't convinced it was entirely true. I'd asked an awful lot of questions today and, like it or not, I knew full well that I was up to my neck in the murder of Christine Montague.

I tried not to think of her still lying in her room when I

passed the closed door. I was walking right past death and could be hot on the heels of the person responsible for it.

I walked down the dead end corridor, wondering what I was going to find waiting.

A closed door was not what I'd expected. I hesitated, wondering if I was going crazy or if there was something paranormal going on. I only ever contemplated it when I was alone in the dark, and I quickly shook the idea from my head. It was while I was pursuing these thoughts that I heard the same sound of footsteps - only this time they were walking on the other side of the door. On a whim, I reached out and pressed down the handle. Jack had told me that the door was locked with no way through, but the handle compressed and I found myself in another long, empty corridor. Someone had found a way to get through - locked, or not. I bit my lip, wondering if this was how the killer had got away. Was there another person in here with the group?

I followed the sound of the footsteps, wondering where they would lead. I'd never wished for a mobile phone with its comforting light (not to mention call function) more than I had in this moment, but all the same, I pressed on. I wanted to know the truth.

A cool breeze brushed against my face and I felt the chill of the night air. Somehow this corridor led outside. The sound of the footsteps had disappeared but I pressed on, feeling my own heartbeat resounding through my chest.

I continued through the darkness, fearing that at any second I would bump into the someone, or something, that I'd been pursuing. The footsteps had stopped, but might the person have heard my own steps and be waiting for me in the darkness? I tried to reassure myself that all people were afraid of what lurked when there was no light, but deep inside, I was sure that there were some who felt more at ease in the dark than in the light. It covered their ill intentions.

My outstretched fingers touched nothing and it wasn't long before I became aware that it wasn't quite as dark as it had been. The breeze had got stronger, too. I walked a little more quickly towards the open doorway that led outside, hesitating only when I was just inside of the threshold. Without realising, I'd somehow made my way up to the bunker roof. It was only with hindsight that I remembered the corridors I'd walked along had been sloping upwards. They'd twisted and turned so many times I'd lost track, but I must have climbed a reasonable amount in order to be up here.

More interesting than the roof itself was the dark figure I could see standing on the edge.

"Who are you and what are you doing here?" I called, pleased to hear how steady my voice was considering the circumstances.

The figure turned around. "Who else would be snooping around on the roof at the dead of night? I thought you used logic to draw conclusions," Fergus sniped.

I felt my shoulders slump as they relaxed. "But I heard you snoring in bed!"

"It's a recording on a very old mini-tape player. I brought it with me just in case."

I raised my eyebrows. "Just in case you needed to sneak out at the dead of night?"

"No… just in case something needed recording. I always knew I was going to use it to sneak out late at night."

I considered this new information.

"Before you even think of asking the question 'was I in my bed last night' the answer is yes, of course I was," Fergus told me patiently.

I tried to recall if I had actually seen him last night and thought that I had. "You stayed in your bed all night?" I wanted to be sure.

"Of course I did. I needed to make sure I got my rest… in preparation for tonight."

I walked over to join Fergus on the edge of the bunker roof, feeling resignation wash over me. He had that effect. "Are you going to tell me just what we're doing on the roof?"

"Signalling," Fergus said, flashing a torch and a mirror at something unseen up in the sky.

"You're trying to communicate with flying saucers," I said, remembering something similar being written in the *Close Encounters of the Seventh Kind* book I'd been reading.

Fergus pulled a face. "Please don't call them that, it's so crass. But essentially, yes. That's what I'm hoping. There's a good reason why this place has been impossible to access for so long. They're hiding something here at Fennering Bunker, and tonight I'm going to find out what it is."

"What exactly are you expecting to find?" I was genuinely curious.

Fergus lifted one shoulder and then the other. "I'm not actually sure. It's like I said to you earlier, this sort of thing isn't really my bag. I'm a minerals and ancient dark energies kind of guy. Extraterrestrials are way too mainstream, but I'm never one to say no to an opportunity, so here I am. There are two prevalent theories about the bunker. The first is that the mysterious owner, and, or, the military are still hanging onto the remnants of the craft that crash-landed here back in the fifties - which is why this place is shut up so tightly, but run with such limited personnel."

I silently acknowledge that he was right about the personnel. There was no one guarding the gate out front but you certainly couldn't get in or out without ending up in some serious and potentially fatal trouble. Razor wire, electric fences, landmines, sharp pointed objects - the bunker's perimeter had it all.

"What's the second theory?" I asked, but I had a feeling I was already watching it.

Fergus waved his mirror at me. "For some reason, this site is a hot spot for UFOs. It's likely that they have some kind of special interest in it. I'm hoping that signalling might draw something here."

We both looked up at the distant stars in silence, and for just a moment, I wondered. Even though I prided myself on being a scientist at heart, all of the best scientists were those who had dared to wonder, those who had considered possibilities that no one else had. When Joseph Lister had put forward the idea that an antiseptic approach to surgery, which included washing hands before operating on patients, could save lives, he had been ridiculed. It was only further on down the line that we looked back in horror at the lack of understanding our ancestors had shown when it came to what was responsible for illness, disease, and infection. I was certain that one day our future selves would look back on some of the practices we conducted now and be equally aghast at our lack of understanding.

Still. There was no way I was going to start chasing aliens.

"Don't most alien sightings turn out to be secret military jets?"

"They don't ever turn out to be secret military jets because the military never admits to having craft like the ones that people report," Fergus corrected.

"Because the military would want to keep their secret projects a secret in the interests of national security," I surmised.

Fergus sighed. "No. It's because they're messing around with alien technology."

I looked at Fergus, who was still flashing his messages at an empty sky. "You really were in bed last night? You didn't climb out of the window?"

"You know I didn't kill Christine Montague. I had no reason at all to do it," Fergus said, already frowning at the implication.

"I don't know... maybe it was an alien sacrifice," I tried to joke, but Fergus' frown only deepened further.

"Sacrifices are for ancient gods and demons, not aliens. Don't be so crude." He kept his eyes fixed on the distant stars. "It's like I told you - I was sleeping in preparation for tonight. Everyone expects you to make your move on the first night, so I always make it on the second."

I thought about that for a bit and concluded the evidence showed he was correct. Christine had been killed the first night we were stuck in the bunker together, and Fergus had picked a much quieter night to go walkabout. "Too bad. You might have seen the killer," I commented,

Fergus shrugged. "You actually did see them running away from the scene of the crime, but it hasn't helped you to get any closer to the truth, has it?"

There was something in his words that suddenly struck me. Running away from the scene of the crime. I'd been assuming that the person I'd seen rushing down the corridor had been the one responsible for the murder. But what made me so sure of the timeline I'd constructed in my head?

I stood at the edge of the roof and went back through the events of the previous evening in chronological order. First, I'd woken up 2:10 a.m. when there'd been the loud bang. I'd poked my head out when Lorna had come and asked if everything was okay. A female voice had replied that they'd seen a spider which had startled them into breaking a mug. I'd made the assumption that it had been Christine talking, but could I really be sure it had been her voice? Next, I'd heard some muffled thumps and Sylvia had screamed, before her door had slammed. I'd looked out and had seen the figure run down the corridor. Jack had arrived a moment later - which did make me think he wasn't the person I'd seen running away. Not unless he possessed super speed. The next day we'd discovered that the murder weapon had been abandoned in Sylvia's knitting bag - presumably where it had been dropped by the killer. Sylvia's window had been open and Christine's had been, too, when we'd found her body the next morning. I'd hypothesised that the killer had gone from one room to the other using the windows. It would explain why Christine's door had been locked from the inside.

When was the last time Christine had definitely been alive? Tanya had knocked on her door at around ten before going to bed. She'd then had a conversation with Christine, although I assumed it hadn't been a long chat, due to Tanya describing Christine as 'not too happy to see her'. That was the last time anyone was admitting to having seen Christine alive. I'd assumed that the stabbing had taken place right before the person had run from the scene - even the smashed alarm clock was frozen in time at the same moment I'd woken up to the great commotion - but what if it had happened earlier? And if it had... what did it change?

I considered the conundrum of the window climbing. To my knowledge, there were no ladders on site. Or at least - none that were accessible to the guests. I'd concluded that the person doing the climbing in and out must be able-bodied enough to haul themselves through a window without the aid of a ladder. That certainly wiped a few suspects off the list.

I shut my eyes for a moment, standing in true darkness whilst I felt the vast empty silence of the night around me. *Did the killer really come in through Christine's window and then do the same with Sylvia's room next door?* I asked myself and ran several possible turns of events through my head. I may not have a chemistry lab at my disposal, but I knew that - once you eliminated all of the impossible scenarios - the one left, however improbable, must be the one that was true.

My mind drifted back to the tragic case of Elliot Harving. I opened my eyes and looked at the stars and slowly, but surely, a lot of things started to fall into place.

"Did you see that?" Fergus asked, breaking into my silent reverie.

I blinked and looked at him.

His shoulders slumped. "Typical. The one time there's actually something to see... look!" He pointed up at the sky and I followed his finger. Out in amongst the bank of stars something blinked in an admittedly similar rhythm to the flashing Fergus had been making.

"It's probably an aeroplane or a satellite," I said, reaching for the most logical explanation.

Fergus shook his head and did some more signalling.

"Is it a message?" I asked, out of curiosity.

"Heck if I know. Never bothered to learn Morse code."

I opened my mouth and then shut it again, looking at Fergus with sudden fondness. He was an endless source of frustration for me, but he also had his moments. Deep down, I still wasn't convinced that the conspiracy theorist was as kookie as he claimed to be, but I was sure that one day he'd get serious, or he wouldn't. And either way was just fine with me.

"So... you saw off that Rich guy pretty effectively," Fergus commented when silence had fallen for a few moments. "Don't know how he ever thought he had a chance with you. Not with those buck teeth."

I frowned. "He doesn't have buck teeth!"

Fergus made a sound of disbelief. "Are we talking about the same guy? He's got more in common with a chipmunk than a human being."

I shook my head and smiled. Rich definitely didn't have

bad teeth or anything else bad about him. I just wasn't interested.

"What about Tanya? She's got a thing for you, hasn't she?" I wasn't sure why I phrased it as a question - it was achingly obvious.

"Oh, that. After you left the dining room she came over to me and I told her that it would never work. My only great love in life is a love of finding the truth." He stared dramatically off into the distance whilst I quietly snorted. Talk about cheesy! He shot me a sideways look. "Anyway, she and Rich seemed fairly okay comforting each other when I left the room. So there is that…"

"It'll be good if one or two of us come away with something worth having after this crazy course."

"I thought it would be a good present," Fergus said, a little disappointedly.

I bit my tongue, feeling bad for a second before I remembered. "You just wanted to come to look for alien activity. I was your plausible cover story!"

Fergus grinned. "Let's say it was fifty-fifty. I really did think you'd like the course. Haven't you learned anything here?"

I considered. "I think I have," I confessed, realising it was true. The interactive videos had been great. Although there was no 'live' interaction, the programmed responses were able to correct a multitude of mistakes and help you if you asked. I assumed that, if the course were to run in the long term, it would be more cost effective than employing tutors each time. It also meant that multiple locations could be used to create a franchise. I definitely saw the business potential, although I was less sure about the high pressure and extreme nature of some of the lessons we'd learned.

"It's all supposed to make you remember it better - having to perform under pressure. You'll be the best flower arranger around when we get out of here," Fergus assured me.

"You won't be too bad yourself," I told him, surprised to discover that I was telling the truth. Fergus had started with less than zero experience and had displayed no enthusiasm whatsoever, but even so, he had learned, and his arrangements had improved.

He frowned. "Against my will! I've done everything I can to not learn anything."

"But it happened anyway. Tough luck. Maybe you can help me out with wedding flowers in the future?"

"Only if you want them covered in glitter, bows, and all things tacky," Fergus warned. "This is the first and last time that I'll be messing around with flowers."

I poked his arm. "You never know, it could be useful someday. What if there was a conspiracy theory about a genus of plant that caused minerals in the soil to turn people into zombies? This could be useful stuff to know!"

"I'd be able to arrange the zombie flowers. Fantastic." Fergus said, making his voice drip with sarcasm. "Anyway, I've got you to help me out with any mineral analyses I need doing. And also that theory is completely ridiculous."

I raised my eyebrows. "How so?"

"Soil minerals are highly unlikely to cause any zombie-like effects in humans or animals. Those substances tend to be caused by synthetically derived stimulants, which cause psychosis and hyperactivity - that can have the effect of making the user walk, run, or even drive without their full knowledge."

I threw Fergus an impressed look. I'd been testing him and he'd actually displayed some decent scientific knowledge.

"Also, something like that would be simple to prove, and therefore wouldn't be a theory I'd have anything to do with.

Unless the government came along to try to hush it up. Then, in the interest of truth, I would be interested." He looked at me and grinned sheepishly. "I kind of talked myself back into that one, didn't I?"

Fergus cleared his throat. "You know, it's been a while since we've hung out like this. How has your business been going? It looked good when I came to visit you. The new house and land is working out for you?"

I nodded. "Everything's been great. Nothing's killed my flowers this time around and business has been really promising. People really are starting to turn their noses up at goods which have been shipped halfway around the world when they have some excellent options on their doorstep. Especially with the political situation what it is right now." We both pulled faces at each other. "I know it's a bit insular to only look at my own business and live in my own little world, but things are going great. I've earned enough money to not have to worry too much over the winter. This year, I may even be able to eat something other than beans on toast," I joked.

Fergus nodded understandingly. "I've always felt fortunate that I like beans on toast."

I shot him a sideways look. I wasn't going to take the bait and ask again about Fergus' primary income source - especially when my instincts told me that Fergus liked keeping it a secret to annoy the curious. I certainly didn't get the sense that he was hard up, but I also wasn't sure why that was the case.

"I know it's none of my business... but after you left, Rich said something about you still being hung up on whatever last guy you were with. I just thought you should know."

"Did you jump to my defence?" I asked, tongue firmly pressed into my cheek. I was a grown woman and could handle a little bit of sniping behind my back - especially when I knew it was just a rejected man licking his wounds.

"I, uh, might have been distracted by dessert."

I rolled my eyes. "I'd have thought you'd be too full of cake to have dessert."

"That would be impossible," Fergus jovially replied.

We looked at the stars in silence before I finally decided to speak. I hadn't really shared my true feelings with anyone about what had happened with the man whose name I avoided speaking, but now, underneath a carpet of celestial balls of burning gas, it felt like the right time.

"My ex-boyfriend George broke up with me because I was too focused on work and not focused enough on him. I didn't take it well," I said, remembering back to my time spent working at the London laboratory with him. "To be honest, I felt that it wasn't fair. He was just as dedicated to his career as I was, and yet, I was the one being blamed for focusing too much on it. At the time, I put it down to him being sore that I'd landed a promotion and he was suddenly effectively junior to me. I thought he couldn't handle it."

"It sounds to me like you probably hit the nail on the head," Fergus commented.

I tilted my head from side to side. "Looking back, I think he might have had a point. I **was** trying to get ahead of him - ahead of everyone. I'd been competing ever since I'd been at school and I just carried on competing - even to the point where I was determined to beat the man I thought I was in love with."

"I bet he wouldn't have felt the same way if he'd got the promotion."

I smiled at Fergus' loyalty. "You're right, but that doesn't excuse my own actions. Looking back, I'm not even sure why I was so focused on it. I like chemistry and I'm ambitious, but what was it all for? I was always going to be another cog in the machine. It's different now. It's my own business and I can see the impact I have on people's lives. Flowers equal happiness. I'm not saying that my chemistry work was useless, but it's nice to not be so removed from the impact you have on the world. And it's nice to choose exactly what impact that is," I said, remembering the fertilisers I'd spent so long analysing and helping to formulate. At the time, it had simply been chemicals mixing together to get a desired result. Now I looked at the potential environmental implications with horror. I knew firsthand what poisoned soil could do to plants and, if you asked Fergus about it, to people, too.

In the end, I knew I would be thanking George for opening my eyes to the truth. It had been hard when I'd left my job in London and settled for a more rural laboratory - all to get away from him and the woman he'd clearly been able to focus on at the same time as both his work and his relationship with me. When I'd started growing flowers and had realised it was something I loved doing - the first thing I'd really loved - it had changed everything. Without George breaking up with me, I wasn't sure I'd have ever found the courage or the drive to make the change. "I'm just not ready for someone else. I still have a lot to do," I said, condensing my feelings into two sentences.

Fergus nodded. "I get it. When you need someone they'll be there. Just keep doing what you're doing. It seems to be going great!"

"Apart from the murders," I muttered.

Fergus shrugged. "You seem to handle those pretty well, too."

I shook my head, I didn't want to have to handle anything like that, but trouble did seem to have a way of finding me. "Not Christine. I'm just not sure..." I said, faltering. My thoughts were still moving around. I had an idea or two, and I thought I'd uncovered the motive, but there were still too many moving pieces. I needed to have them all in place if I wanted to get the killer to confess. As soon as we were out of the bunker, I was sure that there'd never be any headway made into the case. We would all be investigated and asked for our eyewitness accounts, and the jumbled story would obscure the truth. It was just as the killer had intended.

"Hey! There it is again!" Fergus pointed up to the night sky where something was indeed flashing. "How do you explain that, eh?" he said, voice filled with triumph.

"There are any number of explanations for that phenomena. Satellites, aircraft, disturbances in the atmosphere creating the illusion of flashing. There could also be marsh gas causing unusual lights in the sky."

Fergus spluttered. "Marsh gas! You'll consider marsh gas but not the possibility that there are aliens out there? Real aliens, who are signalling to us here down on earth? Doesn't it make you feel tiny?"

I opened my mouth to resume the debate but shut it again. Instead, we stood in the darkness watching the distant blinking light and I reflected that, whatever it was, it did make one feel small when you thought about space and everything it contained.

Even when we felt that our struggles were too much for us to cope with, the universe was a big enough place to hold everyone's problems and carry on - just the same as it always had. It was certainly something that the person responsible for the death of Christine Montague should have considered before delivering their revenge.

10

POISON AND PUNISHMENT

The next morning Fergus woke up looking none the worse for our late night stargazing session. I rolled out of bed looking exactly like I'd had about two hours of sleep over the past two nights - which was fairly close to the truth. My auburn hair was lank. I was glad I'd got rid of Rich the previous day because I sincerely doubted he'd have wanted to pursue me today. I glanced at the time on the little alarm clock and sighed. Twelve more hours and we would be out of here. Would the identity of the killer escape with us? I'd decided last night it wasn't going to happen. I was going to figure out the truth - the whole truth. Someone needed to answer for Christine's death. I was hoping that today would be the day that the killer let their act slip.

We ate our breakfast in a subdued sort of quiet. Today we wouldn't be late for our challenges and I knew that most of us would be grateful when they were over. All the same, I couldn't help thinking that we'd been brought together, a group of people who didn't have much in common other than an interest (Fergus excepted) in flower arranging. I couldn't shake the feeling that, were it not for the suspicion the murder had sown among us, we might have ended with fond memories. Perhaps we'd even have found friendship. I had a sneaking suspicion that the course designer had wanted it that way. No matter what little you might have in common with your course mates, being put through situations that required you to work as a team and succeed as a team drew you together. It was part of our human condition.

Jack led us off to the first room to begin the day's challenges. As we were walking down a long corridor with a light at the end, I reflected on the master keys that had been found in Sylvia's room. Did I still think it was plausible that one of our guides was involved in the murder? Even if I decided to believe their claims that the key set was stolen, it would imply that someone had prior knowledge about where that key set would be left, perhaps intentionally... No matter what the truth was, I was certain that the dropped keys had been a mistake. They weren't left to frame the guides, who had otherwise been left out of being framed. I was sure that the keys were an important factor in figuring out the truth of what happened to Christine Montague.

I was still mulling over everything I knew when the corridor ended and I found myself in a beautiful greenhouse. It took me by surprise. The bunker was many-faceted. This area of the concrete structure was somewhere I hadn't viewed, either from the front or the side. Upon further observation, it became clear why. We were surrounded on all sides, but the light shone down from above and bounced off the bright white concrete walls, that had clearly been painted to encourage sun into the greenhouse. The greenhouse itself was remarkable. The glass looked old and there were decorative curls of hand-hammered metal all over the interior. I wasn't exactly a greenhouse expert, considering that my own 'greenhouses' were just hastily thrown together polytunnels. But I knew that this place was something old enough to be victorian. Put simply - greenhouses simply weren't made this way anymore. I spared a thought to wonder what had come first - the greenhouse or the bunker - and then I spared another several thoughts to wonder just why there was a greenhouse at the centre of a military bunker.

Fergus sidled up to me. I somehow knew that he was going to give me an answer. Probably not the right one, but an answer all the same. "This is curious, isn't it? Almost as if it were built to house and examine life forms brought to the earth by alien vessels."

"It might also have been utilised to test plants for possible military applications," I suggested.

Fergus looked at me with his mouth hanging open. "Did you just suggest a conspiracy theory?"

I blinked at him. "I have no idea what you're talking about."

"But!" Fergus tried to say, but I shushed him when the screen rolled down from the ceiling and Emilia appeared.

"Good morning everyone! I trust all ten of you and your helpful guides slept well?" A wince travelled around the group as everyone was reminded our number had diminished. "Today, we are gathered in the orangery - a remarkable greenhouse that dates back before the erection of Fennering Bunker. When the land was purchased by the government with the intention of creating a military facility it was a condition of the planning permission that the greenhouse was preserved. What you see here is that preservation in practice. In many ways, the bunker has shielded the greenhouse from deterioration by protecting it from the elements with its concrete walls. The angles of the surrounding walls and their reflective paint have always ensured that the orangery remains filled with light and the plants within flourish. Since the military moved on and the site became privately owned so many years ago, the greenhouse has sadly remained empty for the most part. This course has returned it to its former glory. If you look around, you will see a plethora of plants and flowers. The sharp-eyed amongst you will probably have noted that not all of the plants here are native to Britain, and there are some which are flowering out of season." She nodded understandingly. "I know yesterday we focused on the merits of seasonality and the wonderful variety our native country has to offer when it comes to flower choice, but there are also merits to greenhouses. To give an example, British blooms aren't known for their dazzling brilliance in the winter months, but many varieties of orchids will do very well in the greenhouse and give you a focal point for a winter arrangement. That brings us nicely onto today's challenges, the theme for which is sculpture. You have one hour to pick some appropriate flower choices and make a sculptural arrangement suited to a high-class event, or one that would make a simply stunning home centrepiece. Examples will be left on the screen. As always, place your finished arrangements on the table for judging. Good luck!"

"They always start the first challenge so nicely, don't they?" Lady Isabella commented out loud before sweeping off to peruse a row of indoor lilies.

"Was it just me, or did she hesitate after she said today's theme would be 'sculpture'?" I asked Fergus out of the corner of my mouth.

"Look who's being paranoid now," was all he said in response, before mincing off with his choice of vase. I noted, with some surprise, that he hadn't picked a horrible one.

I walked around the greenhouse, taking in the beautiful gerberas and the striking greenery. The first challenge of the day was always the easiest. I found myself relaxing as I inspected a row of slipper orchids.

"Lovely, aren't they?" Sylvia said, looking up at me. "I do

think it's a little wasteful for us to cut them though. Some of these orchids look very fancy to me. But... I am certainly not an orchid expert." She smiled and I smiled back at the woman who'd found a blood-covered weapon in her knitting bag and had quite literally written the book on poisonous plants.

"Don't worry about them. They're easy as pie to grow, if you treat them nicely. Even the supermarkets sell them. A lot of these orchids were brought over from India back when colonisation was all the rage." Eamon raised his eyebrows a little. "There were a lot of new plants that brightened up the aristocracy's gardens in those days. I'll bet that's why the course organiser put these orchids in here as a nod to when the greenhouse was first in use. That there is an aeride - more commonly known as a fox brush orchid."

"I had no idea," I humbly confessed. Most of my own flower growing used native plants because it... well... it felt more British! However, my mind was being opened to these more exotic varieties. Especially when they grew so well and weren't actually imported.

"Well, it's my area of speciality! Asian plants and all that, you know. I lecture on it. It's amazing what we all tend to take for granted without realising the actual origins. Did you know tea plants were brought over from India and went on to flourish in Britain? Camellia sinensis, that is - not assamica."

"I did," I confessed, having had to look that one up myself when I'd been left a pair of tea trees to care for after Jim Holmes had died.

"Oh. Well there you go then," Eamon said, the wind taken out of his sails. "You folks need to get started on your arrangements. An hour isn't long, and you know what tends to happen when our work doesn't come up to scratch." He made some harrumphing noises and then wandered off again.

I reached out and snipped a particularly beautiful orchid, hoping that Eamon was right about them being common and not too tricky to grow. All I knew about orchids was that they were fickle creatures and those that were truly challenging to grow could be very expensive. And if you were fool enough to buy them they'd definitely die on you. Every time someone brought me one of those supermarket orchids I always felt a stab of panic, knowing it was already living on borrowed time. I may be good at growing flowers outside, but houseplants were a different matter.

Still… whilst I wasn't holding out any hope of ever being able to grow orchids, perhaps I could find some inspiration in this greenhouse and transfer it to some cut flower choices of my own. I took my time, selecting a few brightly coloured orchids before moving on to some beautiful peace lilies that were in full bloom.

"You'd be amazed how many houseplants are poisonous." Sylvia had dogged my footsteps ever since we'd been approached by Eamon.

"Oh?" I said, wondering if this was leading somewhere. Somewhere like a confession.

"That peace lily is a good example. The sap can irritate your skin, so watch out. Also, there's that innocuous little shrub over there, the Jerusalem Cherry. People buy it to add a little pop of colour in the winter when it fruits. I'm sure you'll have seen it in garden centres. The problem is, the fruit is poisonous. Cats, dogs, and children have all made the mistake of trying the inviting looking fruit. Fortunately, although it is a relative of deadly nightshade, it's not one of the really nasty ones. So long as treatment is given in time and the symptoms are recovered from, most people are just fine in a few days." She smiled brightly at me.

I silently made a note to check all houseplants gifts people thoughtfully bought for me in the future with great care. Diggory wasn't exactly discerning when it came to what he ate, and I'd never forgive myself if my dog was poisoned because of me.

We found the men gathered around a whole section of greenery.

"I cannot wait to get a takeaway as soon as we're out of here," Rich was saying to Fergus, who nodded ardently in agreement.

"Diana! Come on over here and smell this. Tell me what it reminds you of," Fergus said holding out a leaf-covered stem.

"It's a curry plant," I said, guessing based on the takeaway remarks and the fact that Eamon had already mentioned the greenhouse was full of plants with Asian origins.

Fergus pouted. "Show off. Do you think you can grow me some? Homemade is always best when one is trying to watch one's figure." He patted his belly and looked sideways at the very in-shape Rich.

"Of course," I said, knowing Fergus didn't mean a word of it. I looked down at the vase he held in his hand and felt my eyebrows shoot up. "That looks like it's ready to be judged!"

"Yours isn't too shabby either," Fergus said, giving me a friendly nudge. "Shall we?"

I smiled at him and together we walked over to the judging table both, for a moment, forgetting what we were caught up in the midst of. I hope that when I looked back on this crazy course I'd gone on with Fergus this would be the memory that jumped out at me. This and gazing at distant flashing stars.

It just went to show that even in the face of something terrible, there was always something good to be found, if you were willing to open your eyes to it.

We placed our arrangements down and Emilia appeared on screen congratulating us both for passing the challenge.

"Look at that! No smashed vases today. Plus, yours has fruit on it! That is a nice touch," he reached out to pluck an early-fruiting Jerusalem Cherry.

"Don't be stupid," I said, slapping his hand down. "Honestly, if I weren't around, you'd have poisoned yourself several times over. You're lucky I bothered to learn about edible plants." The smile slid off my face.

"What? What is it?" Fergus asked, his face creasing with concern.

"I know the answer. I know who was responsible for Christine's murder, and I think I have a good idea of why they killed her."

Right behind us there were more sounds of cheerfulness as everyone was congratulated on their finished arrangements. A buzzer sounded and the greenhouse door slid open.

I walked through, my mind heavy with the knowledge that I knew the identity of the killer.

"Well, who the heck is it?" Fergus hissed in my ear.

The door slid shut behind us. I ignored him. In my head, I was going over and over the possibilities, double checking and triple checking. But there could be no mistake. I was right.

A screen slid down and this time Damien greeted us on-screen. "Well done! It is my pleasure to introduce the penultimate challenge to you. I'm sure you're terribly disappointed that there are only three challenges on our final day..." He paused, presumably to let any predicted bitter laughter subside. "However, these final two challenges will combine all that you have learned and use teamwork to succeed, thus finishing as we started - together. Out in the world beyond these walls, there will always be competition, but in here, you have learned the value of shared knowledge and cooperation."

I noticed there was a certain amount of eye-rolling travelling around the room. What were we, children who needed our hands held? *Although... children seldom run round killing people,* I silently amended.

"This penultimate challenge is one I hope you will find fascinating. It takes the importance of having good taste that we covered on day one and combines it with seasonality, reflected in the abundance of the flowers you have to choose between, and then, finally, we will be using these skills to create sculptural forms." There was a quiet whirring sound as several strangely shaped pieces of florist's oasis rose up into view. "Your challenge is to produce ten funeral wreaths," Damien announced with a lot of exuberance.

I looked at the row of green foam and felt something twist in my stomach. It was certainly morbid to be making funeral wreaths when one of our number had so recently died. Especially when I knew her killer was right here among us.

"Here are some examples to get you on the right track. This is a group challenge, so feel free to work on them together, or divide and rule. You have one hour before we move on to your final challenge. Good luck!" Damien disappeared from the screen and instead we were shown a static image of funeral wreaths, provided for our inspiration.

It was inspiration enough for me. I stepped in front of the screen and faced the group I'd worked alongside for the past two-and-a-bit days. A couple of people glanced up and fell silent when they saw the expression on my face. It wasn't long before the entire group was quiet and watching me.

"I think it's time we find out the truth about who is responsible for the death of Christine Montague," I announced.

If it were possible, the silence got even more silent. No one moved a muscle.

"Spit it out then! Who's the killer?" Eamon asked, looking half-enthralled, half-appalled by this shocking turn of events.

I tilted my head at him. "I believe that there's a very good chance that it was you, Eamon. Or at least... you supplied something that made everything else possible."

"Me? That's ridiculous!" he protested as the others drew back from him.

"Allow me to explain. At first, I thought it was Sylvia who had poisoned Christine's tea. The bitter smell of the tea was what first made me suspect poison - and a natural one at that. Poisonous plants often taste foul to alert the unwary eater that they are, in fact, poisonous. However, someone had clearly tried to cover up the taste with the strong-smelling chai. I examined the teabag, but chai is made up of a mix of spices and tea leaves, so it was hard to pick out the poisonous element by sight. It was only today that I realised the identity of the extra ingredient, and it was only because of something you said, Eamon."

Eamon kept his face a mask of bafflement.

"Sylvia wrote the book on poisonous plants, but she wrote it on poisonous plants of the British Isles. I wracked my brains to come up with a British plant that might have caused Christine to remain subdued and then pass away without a struggle - prior to the attack that happened just after her death. I couldn't think of anything that would do that. However, an expert on Asian plants would know about the Indian suicide tree. It is a tragic favourite of those seeking a simple way to die in India. Consumption of the fruit causes the consumer to fall into a coma and then their heart simply stops beating. The seeds of the othalanga fruit have long been used in murders and are probably responsible for many undetected crimes because the cause of death is wrongly attributed to heart failure. I took one of the pieces in the teabag to be nutmeg, or cinnamon bark, but I studied the tree and its deadly harvest long before I was ever interested in growing flowers. It was a potential candidate for a natural insecticide one farm commissioned my laboratory to research for them. It would also account for the choice of a heavily spiced chai. I remember as part of my research, I learned that many poisoners use chilli to cover up the bitter taste of the kernels, but I bet a ground solution mixed with spiced tea would have the same effect with equally successful results."

"You've got no proof," Eamon said. "From where I'm standing, you're the one who knows all about the othal-whatever fruit." He tried to cover up his perfect pronunciation halfway through, but that just made it look as though he was overcompensating. Which he certainly was. Eamon was no hardened killer. He'd never expected to be called out on his contribution to murder, and he'd never envisaged having to defend himself.

"There's proof in the teabag… which is going to remain in that room until the police arrive and they can do their own analysis."

"You could have tampered…" Eamon spluttered, forgetting that the evidence would also be found in Christine's digestive system now that a forensic pathologist would know what to look for.

"In answer to your second point, I have already admitted my prior knowledge of the othalanga fruit and its poisonous element, cerberin. However, there is nothing that ties me to Christine Montague, or Elliot Harving. The same, I think, cannot be said of you."

"I'd never met Christine until the start of this course!" Eamon frowned at me but I could see sweat forming on his neck in spite of the chill in the air. He knew I'd got him.

"I think that may be true. However, I do think you'd met Elliot Harving. In fact, I believe you tutored him during his university years."

Eamon's mouth opened and shut. "I have a lot of students who go on to do great things. I couldn't possibly say…"

"I'm sure a quick check of university records will be able to clear up whether or not you had any contact with Elliot Harving."

Colour crept up the side of Eamon's neck. "That doesn't mean I killed anyone! Even if I did teach Elliot, why on earth would I have wanted to poison Christine Montague?"

"Because you believe that she was responsible for Elliot Harving's death."

A tiny flash of victory danced in Eamon's eyes. "But I never even met Christine Montague! Why would I suddenly meet a woman and decide that she was guilty of a crime? All I know is that the couple responsible, the sculptors, were convicted and punished for their act of sabotage. Even if Christine Montague was somehow involved, how would I, a humble university lecturer, be able to find out anything about the inner workings of the garden design world, or Christine Montague's mind?"

I nodded. "It is unlikely that you personally would have been able to find out anything more about a case that even the police were hoodwinked into believing that they'd solved. But Rich would definitely have been able to uncover that information from his position as Christine's PR guru. When exactly did you start working for Christine?" I directed the question the young South African's way.

Rich blinked, but his smile never faltered. "Did you just imply that I'm somehow involved in this? You just told us all that Eamon was the one who did it."

"I believe Eamon was the one who poisoned the tea, but I don't believe he climbed in and out of two windows, and he certainly didn't singlehandedly inflict all of those stab wounds in Christine's back. At first, they confused me because they varied in depth hugely. Some never pierced the skin and some thrust in deep. I wondered at first if there were two forks being used and the left hand of the attacker was weaker than the right, but I think we all know that there was only ever one fork, and I don't think it probable that a killer in a murderous rage would pause to switch hands halfway through."

The meaning of what I was suggesting hung heavy in the air. Now the group moved away from Rich as well as the ostracised Eamon.

Rich cleared his throat. "I don't think I have to tell you when I started working for Christine…"

He meant it as in 'it's confidential' but I deliberately took it a different way. "You're right - you don't have to tell me. I believe it was soon after the incident that ended in Elliot's death. You were both of a similar age. I know that doesn't mean you must have known each other, but I think you did." I waved a hand to show it wasn't important if he told me the truth or not. "I believe you mistrusted the public version of events that led to Elliot's death and you must have also had your suspicions about who was responsible. I'm going to hazard a guess that Elliot mentioned his rivalry with Christine Montague prior to his death, and that was what inspired you, a young and talented PR man, to pursue employment with Christine Montague. You might have suspected that she was involved from something Elliot said prior to his death, but I think you wanted to find out the truth by investigating it yourself."

"And what did I find?" Rich asked, his amusement gone but no sign of a flicker of alarm in his expression. Rich was a tougher nut to crack than Eamon had been.

"I think you found something that made you sure enough

about the truth that you decided to act and deliver the justice that was so gravely misplaced on the innocent sculpting couple." Sylvia's lips puckered for a moment when I mentioned the sculptors. I silently confirmed another theory. "Once you knew the truth, the question was how to go about getting justice for Elliot without, presumably, incriminating yourself." I looked around the room at all of the pale faces. "I suppose you came into contact with everyone else who was involved in the murder of Christine Montague and hatched a plan that would make sure no one was caught. After all, it's not every day that multiple killers convene in order to make a crime appear to be something it is not - the act of a single perpetrator who carried out a random attack motivated by robbery."

"That's preposterous! None of us knew anyone before we all met on this course," Eamon spoke up again, once more looking a tad too satisfied for my liking.

"I think you're telling the truth," I informed him, before I played my ace. It was with a flourish that I turned to face Fergus and asked him an essential question. "Who owns this bunker?"

My conspiracy-minded companion jumped to attention. "Sir Gordon Laird. He's a private man who decided to buy the ex-military base seemingly out of the blue. However, he has military links himself, and I believe it was purchased to conceal evidence of an extraterrestrial landing site…"

I thanked him, deciding to ignore the part where Fergus had got sidetracked. "I think the search for a connection between Sir Gordon Laird and Elliot Harving will be an interesting one for the police to investigate." I paused for dramatic effect. "Unless someone here wishes to enlighten me?" I looked around the room, knowing I had the mystery of Christine Montague's death all but solved.

When no one spoke, I decided to tighten the screw.

"Christine was professionally jealous of Elliot Harving's success and rising stardom. She loved anything sculptural and used sculpture often in her garden designs. With her history of working as a structural engineer, it was her unique selling point. The best garden designers use the best suppliers. I would wager that both Elliot and Christine had commissioned sculptures for the Chelsea Flower Show from John and Winifred Culvert that fateful year. The next part was never witnessed, but I believe that Christine must have sabotaged Elliot Harving's sculpture in some way which resulted in his untimely death. She did it in such a way that only a witness or confidant could prove she was the one responsible - and I think it's probably a secret that she took to her grave. This lack of evidence is why you are all here to get justice for Elliot Harving."

"And for John and Winifred! They would never have hurt a fly and they knew their business well. They had years of life and passion left in them. It was taken from them in that dreadful prison with a sentence they should never have been given. Pneumonia! Pah! It was their broken hearts that killed them – seeing everything they'd worked so hard on crumble to dust. They were shattered by Elliot's death and for them to shoulder the blame on top of that... it was too much!" Sylvia cut in, breaking the silence that had settled over the group. A few accusing eyes landed on her. "I was just friends with them," she finished defensively and then looked at me with a closed expression. She hadn't confessed to anything beyond knowing the sculpting couple, but I'd already guessed it was her connection to the case.

Rich was still shaking his head. "Poison might be one thing, but which of us is supposed to have stabbed her? Her room was locked from the inside! We were all tucked up in bed. According to your own account, and corroborated by Lorna, you heard Christine alive and well at around two 'o' clock that night. It even makes your tea theory sound rather fanciful, doesn't it?"

I allowed the tiniest of smiles to grace my lips. This was something that had stumped me for a while. "It would... if I really had heard Christine. I think she was dead a lot earlier than any of us realised. Someone went in to check that she was unconscious or dead. It was that person who then pretended to be Christine after knocking the incriminating mug over in her room, spilling the poisoned tea. It was an excellent cover and all part of the meticulously conceived plan. However, I do think it was overdoing it a bit to break the alarm clock and arrange the hands at the time she was supposed to have died."

"But I tried the door. It was locked! Who else could it have been but Christine? She would have locked her own door, surely?" Lorna said. I noticed her eyes turned to Jack. He blushed crimson, no doubt remembering the lost master keys.

"It was those master keys, stolen by someone who knew where to look, that let the checker into Christine's room. They knew that whoever came when the mug broke would try the handle when they got no response at first. The idea was that we would all assume her door remained locked from that time onwards and that the intruder could only have come through the window - left carelessly open. As soon as all was quiet again, at planned intervals, all of you crept into Christine's room taking care to be silent - even covering your feet with the thick pairs of socks that a lot of you had in your suitcases to muffle any sound. If you were caught then, it would have been a disaster! But even so, I am sure you each had a plausible excuse as to why you might be wandering around in the middle of the night.

However, you did leave some evidence behind. A jewelled hairpin and a medical bracelet must have both fallen off unnoticed during your individual strikes against the woman who wronged a man and a couple that you all cared about. At first, I believed that evidence was planted to deliberately lead an investigator astray. It was just so obvious! But in the end, it didn't matter either way. You'd already predicted that suspicion may turn on a member of the group and a luggage search must also have been an eventuality you foresaw, hiding various pieces of incriminating evidence in many peoples' suitcases."

"Doesn't that suggest to an investigator that it wasn't a break-in?" Fergus asked, frowning a little at the change of story.

I smiled at him. "I believe the perpetrators wanted to throw in as many red herrings as possible, but yes... in an ideal world, I still think they wanted the mysterious intruder to be culpable. I even think they opted for the military outfit and the phosphorescent glow in order to pique your own interest," I told my companion. "The organiser must have tipped them off that you were coming." I turned back to my stony-faced audience. "After the deed was done, and you'd had your moment of revenge, you each returned to your rooms. Everyone, I think, apart from Tanya and Rich. The military figure was supposed to be assumed to be a male, but upon reflection, I think that Tanya, with a little padding here and there, fits the profile I saw running away. Rich, you told me that one of your hobbies was climbing when you were growing up in Cape Town." I glanced pointedly down at his calloused hands when I said it. Callouses the size of Rich's were not the usual fare for a man who claimed to work solely in PR. "I think you've kept the hobby up and it came in handy for getting out of Christine's window and back into your own without the aid of a ladder. That would allow you to have locked her door from the inside, cementing the idea that the killer entered through the window and left the same way. Sylvia helped, too, by first letting Tanya in and then making sure her window was open. "

Rich shrugged his shoulders, not giving anything away.

"That sounds like utter rubbish to me," Duncan suddenly announced. "I was in the same room as Bella for the whole night. She never left. She doesn't have anything to do with this."

I raised my eyebrows at Bella. Both of us knew that she had indeed left the room and that Duncan was (knowingly or not) lying for her.

"Does he know that you're Elliot's sister?" I asked her. There was a moment of charged silence whilst I kept my expression perfectly blank. It was a stab, if not in the dark, then in a dimly lit room, but I had a hunch I was correct.

When Bella shook her head, the whole house of cards finally tumbled down.

"We weren't together long before we married. I'd already changed my name by then. I didn't want to be the pitied sister of 'that poor man' Elliot Harving for the rest of my life. I wanted to move on and have a normal life," she said, her eyes begging me to understand. "How did you know?"

"Your Kindle case bore the initials 'E.R.H' but when Duncan introduced you as 'Smith' I made the assumption that the 'H' was a maiden name. I looked at your age and made an educated guess that you, an apparently innocent outsider with no connection to the gardening world, must have a connection. Because everyone here has a connection to Elliot Harving."

"I don't. I swear!" Jack said looking anxiously from me to Fergus.

"My apologies. I should have said everyone apart from three course members and your two guides. The guides were supposed to act as witnesses. Their job was to investigate any nighttime disturbances and their investigation would have played perfectly into your plan. I assume the only spanner in the works was when Fergus somehow managed to book us both on a course you'd intended to keep amongst a group of carefully selected people - with no connection to one another beyond professional reputation, and the secret that you all had an axe to grind with Christine Montague."

I glanced at the timer on the wall and noted that the minutes were slipping by. The truth would have to come out soon or all of us would be in for a nasty shock for failing a challenge.

"It's not like anything can be proven," Rich muttered, more to himself than anyone else when no one said a word. "What happens on the retreat, stays on the retreat, right? I say we share the whole truth. Otherwise she is definitely going to go to the police, and she knows enough to get us all." He directed the next comment at me. "We aren't killers. I think you know that already."

"I'm banking on it," I commented. It would be no joke to be stuck, even for a few more hours, with a group of psychopaths willing to cut down anyone in their path, but this whole situation was different. I was certain this unlikely group had been drawn together by some terrible circumstances, which included a gross failing on the part of the justice system. This had been their last resort, and deep down, I believed they were willing to pay for what they had done - no matter the cost.

"Then I think it's time you got your facts straight. No one bothered to before now," Rich continued, ending with a grumble. He looked around the group and received a few nods of approval. "None of us has the whole story, but, prior to this trip, we all harboured strong suspicions that Elliot Harving's death didn't come about the way that the police and the papers claimed it did."

11

THE ART OF DECEPTION

"What made each of you suspect?" I asked. I'd figured out most of their connections to Elliot Harving, but there were still some mysteries I'd been unable to fill in.

"You already worked out that I knew the Culverts," Sylvia spoke up. "I knew their work and knew there was no way they'd have sent a shoddy piece of work out into the world - no matter how overworked the police claimed they were. They only ever took on what they could handle! When John and Winifred Culvert passed away, I was devastated. I dedicated my most recently published book to the couple. That was when Sir Gordon got in contact with me, asking if I believed that the Culverts had been responsible for Elliot's death. I told him that it was about the unlikeliest thing I'd ever heard. We kept in touch and the next thing I knew, he'd somehow found out the truth of the matter. Then it was just a case of what was to be done about it." Sylvia's mouth twisted in discomfort when she said the last part.

"I suppose I will go next," Lady Isabella spoke up,

surprising me. I'd assumed that she wasn't on the course by chance, but I hadn't been able to work out how, exactly, she was connected to a young garden designer.

"My best friend was Elliot's grandmother. The papers didn't say a word when she died so soon after Elliot's death. Doctors just said it was a heart attack that caused her demise, but I know it was a broken heart. She had to watch as her son and his wife dealt with all of the press and the terrible tragedy of losing their son. More than that, she felt as well as any of us that the investigation was shoddy because of the pressure put on the police to find someone responsible. So they jumped to the obvious conclusion and those poor sculptors took the rap." She gave her head a single brisk nod and fell silent.

Tanya shot her a curious look before taking her cue. "I was dating Elliot at the time of his death. We'd only just started going out, but I really cared about him! More than that, he confided in me. He told me that he thought someone was out to get him. Just one week before Chelsea, he told me that he thought someone had poisoned his plants. After some investigation, something was found to be wrong with their water supply – a supply that was reserved for the plants and should not have been contaminated! He never told me what the contaminant was, just that it was plausible that it came from a natural origin... but he was certain it hadn't. It was too much of a happy coincidence for whomever it was that wanted him to fail." I tilted my head in question but Tanya had already read what I wanted to know. "Elliot had enemies. He wasn't a patch on Christine in terms of a cut-throat attitude and reputation within the industry, but he'd learned the hard way that being known as 'nice' never does you any favours."

I silently appreciated that she did have a point there. If

you had to reach for a word like 'nice' to describe someone, it usually meant that they were so devoid of personality, or interest, that there was simply no other word to describe them with.

"Sir Gordon contacted me after I spoke at a memorial service for Elliot that was held for his friends, rather than family. I may have said a thing or two I shouldn't have and caused a bit of bad feeling," she confessed. "But no one there seemed to believe it was anything other than the line they'd been fed! I mean, there was no way. No way that it just happened the way they said it did. You were right, by the way - about the costume. It was a last minute thing. When one of our number couldn't make it, and one of the course guides tried to bring in outsiders, Sir Gordon had to make the final decision. He researched both of you and decided that a cut flower businesswoman and a conspiracy theorist wouldn't harm proceedings. He thought that Fergus might even come up with something wacky to further convolute matters. The military uniform and glow paint was supposed to make you think of aliens, or something." She shrugged and then looked sheepishly at me. "Nothing was ever said about you being some kind of scientist. Sir Gordon should probably have looked harder. I was the one who brought her the tea, by the way. I gave it to her when I told you we had our conversation."

I considered that and found I was pleased I was only known for my flower business. I'd left my old life working in chemistry behind, and while it did come in handy from time to time, I loved my new life and business.

"As you already guessed, I was Elliot's lecturer. He had others whilst studying at Nottingham Trent, but we were really rather close. He was the kind of student who would see me after a lecture to clarify things and ask for more information on a topic. I knew back then that he was a student destined for great things. He had that commitment and drive that can only come from within a person." Eamon shook his head in memory. "To be honest with you, when Elliot passed away I was saddened but had no idea that the story was anything other than the one printed in the papers. I suppose I was sort of headhunted to play my part." His eyes danced nervously as he stopped himself from fully confessing to poisoning Christine - even though I was certain that he'd been the one to supply the poison, if not the one who'd actually taken her the tea. "Anyway, Sir Gordon reached out and asked me if I'd considered that Elliot's death might have been something more than an accident caused by poor workmanship. Until that point, I hadn't even considered it. But he made some excellent points. He promised to keep in touch with me."

Bella cleared her throat and moved forwards. "You already know that I'm Elliot's sister. Sir Gordon got in touch with me after I got myself into trouble trying to look into Elliot's death myself, only during this past year. I kept it quiet because I'd already changed my name and didn't want anyone to know who I was, but I definitely stepped on a few toes when people involved in the investigation realised I was questioning their work. I just…" She sighed. "…I just couldn't accept it was an accident, I suppose. I didn't really have any knowledge about metal-working, or even that my brother had made enemies, I just wanted there to be a better explanation beyond poor craftsmanship and bad luck." Her breath hitched for a moment. "They said Elliot saved a whole bunch of people by pushing them out of the way when that sculpture fell. My brother had his flaws. He was human like anyone else. But when it really mattered, he always did the right thing." She bit her lip. "I just wanted to do the right thing, too." Bella glanced up at her husband who had been pale ever since the truth had started to come out, bit by bit.

"You killed someone!" he said, causing alarm to flash across Bella's face.

"I didn't. Not really," she implored before falling silent.

Rich took a step forward – the last person to speak. Somehow, I knew that it was his story that had brought about all of this.

"Elliot and I were close friends. I first met him as part of a 'young entrepreneurs' programme. The programme paired up ambitious young people, and I guess we were two names out of the hat. The idea was that you shared your ups and downs whilst pursuing your own business or sole enterprise and that you acted as support for each other." Rich's trademark smile slipped a little. "It started out that way for us, but as our success grew in our respective fields, so did our friendship. I was working in Australia when Elliot died, but I knew immediately that something wasn't right. Much like Tanya, Elliot had told me that someone was out to get him. Only, with me he'd shared the name of the person he suspected was responsible for the strange things that kept happening to derail his show garden. Christine Montague. When he died because of that freak sculpture accident, I knew there was something off about it. I'd built my professional reputation up by then, and I also strongly believe that the best way to get the truth is to find it yourself. I contacted Christine Montague offering to be her PR guy by proving that I was infinitely better than the entire agency she'd hired. Once my visa was sorted, I came over and worked for a woman I suspected might have had something to do with Elliot's death." He ran a hand through his tawny hair. "After everything I went through to get that job, it was almost too easy to find out that Elliot had been right all along. Christine figured out pretty quickly that I was the best member of her team, so we worked closely together." He shrugged his shoulders. "I suppose she must have imagined that she was safe to speak plainly to her staff. She used to heavily hint about the lengths she would go to - to not only be the most in demand high-end landscaper out there, but to take out her competition along the way. I guess if I hadn't already had the idea that she'd had something to do with what happened to Elliot, I might have assumed she only meant it figuratively. Even with all of my heart wanting there to be a good reason, one beyond carelessness, for what happened to my friend, I kept an open mind. The closer I got to Christine, the more troubling information I was able to learn. When we were preparing for this year's Chelsea, I found some records from previous years lying on her desk. I looked through and discovered that the year of Elliot's death, she, too, had commissioned reclaimed metal sculptures from the Culverts."

I nodded. I'd been right about that educated guess.

"But it was only when I stumbled upon her original garden design that I discovered something significant. When Christine had first planned her show garden, it had featured a reclaimed sculpture as the centrepiece. In the final design there were just two small sculptures that featured in the garden. I asked Christine why her design had changed, claiming I'd happened upon the file and been curious. She told me herself that the Culverts had refused to take on the commission because they'd already been booked by Elliot Harving to create a centrepiece for his show garden." Rich lifted and dropped his shoulders. "Garden design is more competitive than people imagine. I'm sure it would have been a coup for Elliot to have beaten Christine to the punch. But I believe the Culverts' honour was to be their downfall." He sucked air through his teeth for a moment. "I tried. I tried so hard to find evidence that would bring Christine down, but she wasn't that careless. Christine was paranoid when it came to business - and for good reason. It was only when I pushed to get even closer to her and we actually went out for dinner that I discovered her background in structural engineering. I was actually surprised when she casually dropped it into conversation in the first challenge! Apparently, building things was what led to her appreciation for gardens that had a form and a balance. It had always marked her as different from the rest, who were inspired by the plants they used. That was when I really started to suspect that Christine was behind it - just as Elliot had suspected. Someone trained in structural engineering would have known the weak point in a sculpture, and with two smaller sculptures commissioned by the Culverts, she would have had every opportunity to visit their workshop and sabotage her competitor's centrepiece. But that wasn't what made me certain. It was a different incidence of Christine's brand of foul play. It was another case of her devious nature and she never admitted to any of it, but one comment made prior to Hampton Court Flower Show stuck with me. She'd read in the paper about a horticultural event abroad that had experienced a bomb scare. Something about it struck her as amusing and she shared it with me saying something like 'Wouldn't that be a hoot!'. Then, at the show itself, an unattended suspicious item was reported by an anonymous visitor. It just so happened to be next to a competitor Christine had spent the previous two weeks complaining about. The bomb squad was called in when it looked like the item did have the potential to be explosive. It was only later that the bag was found to contain some of her rival's garden supplies, as well as a small homemade explosive device - making it look like this competitor had problems within her company."

"You think Christine actually made the explosive?" I knew that everyone present strongly believed that Christine had been responsible for Elliot's death, but I wanted to know just how much evidence they possessed. Had they murdered an innocent woman? *Well, not exactly innocent,* I mentally corrected, having deduced from Rich's story that she'd definitely had a mean streak and a ridiculously unsporting approach to business - but that didn't necessarily make her a killer who'd got away with murder.

"I wasn't certain until I heard more about the so-called device. It wasn't really an explosive but some thermite and a little gunpowder to make it go bang. It's simple enough to make if you have access to the materials. The choice struck me - again, it was because of Christine's structural engineering history. She would know how to make, or get, thermite, and she would have known for sure what it would do if it were... say... placed over a weld and ignited by magnesium with a timed trigger so small that the heat of the thermite would completely destroy it."

"Hang on... thermite burns brightly," I said, knowing the way it worked from years spent studying chemistry at university. "If thermite had been ignited at Chelsea Flower Show I'm sure people would have noticed."

Rich inclined his head. "It wasn't actually detonated when anyone would have been around to witness. I think it happened the night before. It would account for the way it made the metal look like a weld failed. Thermite would burn straight through it. The reclaimed metal and the fact it had actually been welded before would have made it appear as though nothing untoward had happened beyond human error. The metal itself couldn't even have been analysed properly because it would have had traces of all kinds of things on it. I mean, these sculptures look like rust-covered relics, tacked together with welds and rivets! It's no wonder that the investigators didn't look very far."

"You're saying that Christine didn't deliberately plan to murder Elliot?" I wanted to get that clear.

Rich looked awkward for a second. "No. But she'd have

known there was potential for people to get hurt – badly hurt! She would have known that thing would fall apart at some point after the thermite had done its work. She just didn't care. The bomb scare was the same. What if someone had picked up that device before the bomb squad got there? The thermite could have ignited and caused a serious injury. Even death!"

"Even though she may never have intended to actually kill Elliot, she never came forward to confess to what she'd done or to get the Culverts out of the mess they were put in," Sylvia pointed out.

"She never showed any remorse for any of her actions," Rich jumped in again. "We gave her one last chance. Christine loved hidden meanings. She used to delight in picking plants that secretly insulted clients she didn't like. That was really as far as her interest in actual horticulture went – the so-called 'language of flowers'. You know the rest. She ignored the warning. We gave her a chance."

I looked around at a face marked by anger and grief. I didn't personally believe that revenge was ever a good idea. Six people had potentially just thrown their lives away to settle a score.

The snapdragons and their hidden meaning of 'deception', marked with the name 'Harving', had been her last chance to tell a truth they all believed she'd been hiding. Christine Montague had tried to seek Fergus' help, but I knew that Fergus had been as repulsed by her as a person as I was. There'd been something rotten about Christine Montague that I thought I'd sensed when I first met her. I was surprised to find myself thinking along those lines. In the past, I would always have discounted anything labelled as a 'gut feeling'. It was hardly an evidence based approach to life, but perhaps I was changing with Fergus' influence. And from our conversation beneath the stars, I thought he might be changing, too.

"There you go. That's the story. As much as you need of it anyway. The question now, is what happens next?" Rich looked sad when he said it, but I felt no aggression from him.

"I'll accept punishment for what I've done. I'd do it again in a heartbeat! She was evil. Pure evil! At least our actions will make people ask the right questions. Perhaps one day the whole truth will be found... somehow," Bella said.

Rich shook his head. "I don't believe it. I spent two years working with that hag and trying to find the truth in the proper way. It doesn't exist. She had too many years of experience at playing these kinds of games. Perhaps someone with more patience might have said that karma would one day catch up with her but I am okay with playing karma's role. I don't mind facing retribution for this."

There were murmurs of assent from around the room.

Duncan coughed, causing everyone to turn and look at him. "I... I think I understand now. I understand more about you," he said, turning to Bella. "I'm so sorry about your brother. I just wish you'd told me. I would have stayed by your side. Always."

"You would?" Bella said, beaming from ear to ear. "Oh... Duncan!" She hugged him close to her.

"It doesn't really seem fair," Jack said, breaking the silence and then blushing when the group's attention rested on him. "It's just... the way I see it, if this is all true, then the woman you killed really had it coming. She was a terrible person and you were all hurt so much by what she did. It makes sense. I'm just saying, it seems super unfair that she got away with it in the first place and that there was nothing that could get her to confess to it all."

"Too bad the law doesn't condone vigilante justice,"

Fergus called from somewhere else in the room. "Trust me on that one…"

I decided not to pry further right now.

"So… I guess we should enjoy our freedom for the last couple of hours," Rich said with a little smile. "You're going to the police, right?" There was a challenge in his voice that I didn't like, but I already knew exactly what he was asking me.

I considered everything and looked around at the group. Everyone seemed to be holding their breath. Was murder still murder if the person really had it coming to them? I knew the answer was yes. And yet, here we were separated from the normal world and perhaps even (momentarily) in charge of our own justice.

I released the breath I'd been holding whilst I thought. "The way I see it, there are two options as to how we can help the police to solve Christine Montague's untimely death. The first scenario is that an intruder managed to break-in to the compound. They picked Christine's room because of its open window. Christine woke up and saw the intruder. The post-mortem will reveal that she actually died of a heart attack. Whilst she was dying from heart failure, her intruder callously stabbed her with a fork, stolen from the property's shed, and then abandoned in the room next door when the callous intruder tried their luck in Sylvia's bedroom, before her scream caused them to flee down a corridor where they somehow made their escape through a door we'd all imagined was locked." I sucked in more air. "Or, you come clean and the truth comes out for everyone." I wasn't sure how the police would go about making a case against six different killers - especially when only one had actually done the killing. And who was to blame for her death anyway? Was it Eamon for supplying the poison or Tanya for taking it in to Christine? This case would be more of a nightmare than the original investigation that the police had bungled so badly. Not to mention there was scant evidence beyond my word, the tainted teabag, and the items we'd taken from the floor. The flowers would be dead and the message lost by now. There would be nothing beyond a vague connection to Elliot Harving to tie any of Christine's killers to the crime. They had been careful to not be in contact with each other prior to this trip and I was sure that Sir Gordon Laird, the man responsible for setting this entire scenario up, would not have held on to any evidence, beyond his launching of the course and his invitations to a select few who had applied - apparently randomly - to attend this exclusive course.

I wasn't sure how the police would ever put the pieces together.

"I vote for option A," Rich said, his dark eyes looking seriously into mine. I thought I saw a flash of regret there and realised his mind was no longer on the murder. I turned away and focused on the rest of the group.

"I don't think it's right for anyone to get into trouble. These people got the justice that they wanted. I think that sometimes the law and what's right don't match up," Lorna spoke up before turning to look at Jack. He merely nodded his agreement.

"Fergus?!" I called, not seeing him anywhere.

"Hmm? Oh, yes, right. Option A sounds like much less hassle. Crimes committed at random are very tough to solve, which means they're dropped quickly. None of us wants to be dragged through the courts…" His voice trailed off. Apparently that was all Fergus had to say on the matter.

"I think we have a consensus," I said, feeling as though a weight had lifted from my shoulders. Looking around, I suspected that I wasn't the only one who felt that way.

"Dash it all! The challenge!" Eamon said, returning us all to the crazy world of extreme floristry with a bump.

A buzzer sounded a second after he said it. We all winced and looked around, wondering what terrible punishment was about to smite us.

"Don't all thank me at once, but haven't we got a final challenge to attend to?" Fergus drawled from the doorway that had just opened up.

There was a moment of stunned silence as everyone looked from Fergus to the judging table at the ten finished funeral wreaths.

"No way," Rich said, saying what we were all thinking.

"While you were talking I realised someone needed to finish the darn things." Fergus shrugged self-deprecatingly when the group belatedly heaped praise on him for his work.

I was last through the doorway into the final challenge room. I hesitated on the threshold next to Fergus. "Are we doing the right thing?" I asked, my eyes searching his face for an answer.

"The right thing is subjective when applied to a question of morality rather than one of science," Fergus said in complete seriousness.

I stared at him and he grinned. "It is quite fun, isn't it? Being the logical one."

I rolled my eyes at him, feeling the strange moment break along with Fergus' false serious veneer. "If that was an impression of me, it was a terrible one."

We looked towards the group, who'd congregated around the table of snacks that had been laid out prior to the next challenge beginning. "In all seriousness, I think we did what was best, given the circumstances. Yes, it would have been better for everyone if Elliot Harving's death had been more thoroughly investigated and Christine had slipped up and been found guilty of her many supposed sabotage attempts -

which I think are all plausible when you add the many unlikely coincidences together," he added, comforting me somewhat. "I'm willing to bet we've spent more quality time with those six murderers than a lot of people spend with them in a year. Do they strike you as evil, or in need of punishment? They've already punished themselves enough ever since their loved ones died. Yes, they acted out of anger and a desire for retribution. I'm not saying they did a good thing, or that it was right, but I also don't think that six lives - eight, if you include poor old Duncan and the man who allegedly set this whole thing up - should be ruined because of the death of a woman who, by all accounts, will not be greatly missed."

"But that doesn't mean there wasn't anything good about her," I protested, trying to say something in Christine's favour.

Fergus' dark eyes drew me in for a second. "You always try to see the best in everyone, even when they're terrible. It will get you into trouble. Sometimes there really is no good in a person. They've gone too far down a track to consider turning back. I think you know exactly what kind of person Christine Montague was." Fergus lightly brushed a hand across my arm, before he went and joined the throng at the snack table. I found I appreciated the effort to continue our conversation for as long as it had lasted - given that I knew he would have wanted to be first to the food. Some things about Fergus would never change, and I wouldn't have it any other way.

My gaze was inexorably drawn back to the row of funeral flowers finished by Fergus and laid out on the table like a final farewell. A shiver crawled up my spine when I thought about the body in the bedroom and the morbid choice of the previous unusual floristry challenge. He would have known that Christine Montague would be dead by this time. Had this challenge been a subtle apology for actions borne out of anger, or had it been a sick joke?

I turned away from the wreaths and was glad when I heard the door slide closed behind me, shutting out the funeral scene. I wanted nothing more to do with death for a long, long time.

12

A TRICKY CUSTOMER

The final challenge was, as promised, a combination of everything we were supposed to have learned on the course. We each had to make two arrangements - a bouquet displayed in a vase and a more sculptural piece, using a block of Oasis we were encouraged to carve ourselves. I sincerely hoped that no one decided to make anything that even slightly resembled another funeral wreath.

At first, we all went about our work in silence, picking the seasonal flowers and greenery for the bouquet or sculptural display and then working on a theme of complimentary colours for the other. After the minutes stretched the first chatters broke out as people began talking amongst themselves. I glanced across at Fergus and discovered he was working on something that didn't look half bad.

"Will you stop looking at me in surprise?" he commented, and somehow, that seemed to open the floodgates of normality. The rest of the surprisingly relaxed challenge harkened back to the way things had been prior to Christine's murder. When we finally lined up our bouquets and displays, I noticed that everyone's looked great - professional, even. Somehow, against all of the odds, we'd learned a lot about flower arranging over these past three days. The course's concept of learning under pressure did seem to ring true.

When Lorna triumphantly pushed the button next to the time lock, it immediately stopped with one hour to go, before letting out a cheerful sounding buzzer and swinging open. I spared a thought about what might have happened if we'd been late, but sometimes it was better to not solve every mystery you came across in life.

As soon as we were out of the course, and reunited with the box of mobile phones that had been left in the first room where we'd first met, Lorna called the police and reported Christine Montague's murder. The police arrived in the next fifteen minutes and the questioning began.

It wasn't too difficult to stick to the story in the end. If it had been an intruder, we would all have known so little anyway. We'd all agreed that smashed cup of tea and the bag should be missing when the police entered the room, but the rest would stay the same. Well - apart from the evidence Fergus and I had already removed!

The police were just beginning to ask some trickier questions about how a potential intruder would be able to access the secure compound when Sir Gordon Laird arrived. He was a large man with an impressive ginger and grey moustache and a refined sense of fashion.

"What's all this to do about then?" he asked after sweeping in and immediately becoming the centre of attention. Nothing in his expression hinted that he had any idea of the happenings at Fennering Bunker, but I knew that he probably had more of an idea of how the pieces fitted together than any of us here. He'd been the one who'd organised the entire murder of Christine Montague.

I suddenly realised that I wasn't sure why Sir Gordon himself had been so interested in Elliot Harving.

The police explained what had happened and then repeated their questions about how an intruder would be able to access the secure compound.

"I can answer that," Sir Gordon said, his face appropriately grave. "I was already on my way here because of a report that the exterior fence had been damaged. With the course due to end, my caretaker was able to inspect the outside and called me immediately. The others have already explained the nature of the course and the banning of all outside communication?"

"Yes, that's very unusual, isn't it?" the lead detective enquired.

Sir Gordon waved a hand in his face. "Not at all. It's scientifically proven! In this day and age it's so easy to be distracted by social media and the internet and whatnot. This course takes all of that away and piles on the pressure. It results in new skills being learned and, most importantly, remembered. I'm as excited as anyone to see the final pieces that the group produced," he said, beaming round at all of us, as if we weren't in the midst of a murder enquiry.

"Jenkins! Did you take down the description of the person that Ms Flowers saw fleeing the scene?" the detective barked, determined to take back control of the situation.

"Yes Sir! Uh... military uniform and glowing."

"Glowing?" The detective fixed me with a look of pure disdain. "I hope you're not suggesting..."

"That it was the work of an extraterrestrial visitor? I'm impressed you know so much about the illustrious history of this bunker," Fergus said, neatly sliding into the conversation at exactly the right moment.

"Preposterous!" The detective squinted at Fergus. "Don't I know you? I feel as though we've met..." He made a humming noise, quite unselfconsciously, as he worked to recall Fergus' face. "I've got it! I've had to caution you for trespassing. Weren't you trying to break-in to this very bunker?!"

Fergus didn't look even slightly abashed. "Yes, but this time, I was invited."

"But you have prior experience!" the detective protested, looking like he believed he was onto something.

"Sirs, if I remember correctly, he failed every time," Sir Gordon jovially contributed. "And he is correct. This time, he was invited."

"I thought this was an exclusive floristry event? Surely you can't have believed that a man who wanted to trespass on your property to hunt for aliens would have any genuine interest?" The detective was growing incredulous.

"I wasn't hoodwinked in the slightest! I knew his companion was a bonafide business woman, and just the sort we wanted to try out the new course, but to be perfectly frank, I wanted someone who was completely uninterested in floristry to be put through their paces. How did you fare in the end, Fergus?"

"He's very good!" I said, unable to hide my smile at Fergus' grudging expression. "I'm considering employing him to make wreaths as an expansion for my business."

"Not for any money!"

"That's very kind of you. I'm sure I could pay you in biscuits?" I said, deliberately misunderstanding him.

Whilst the conversation descended into petty sniping, the police tried to find more answers but were left as at sea as we'd all hoped. There was no mention of Elliot Harving, and I knew there never would be. With no connection to Christine found in the original case there was no chance that a connection would be found in this one. I'd only been able to follow the path of truth myself because of a wilted snapdragon. I knew that now it would be no more than a dead stem with black curled petals. No one would ever find the message written in marker pen and the police would forever search for the mystery intruder who'd committed a murder.

In years to come, I had no doubt that the unsolved mystery of Christine Montague's murder would join the other conspiracy theories that surrounded Fennering Bunker.

"So... did you really feel that you all learned something?" Sir Gordon asked when the police finally excused us all to continue their examination of the scene of the crime.

We all looked round at each other, considering it properly for the first time. All of a sudden, my brain was full of the advice we'd been given on arranging, seasonal flowers, the importance of giving customers what they wanted, but without compromising your own standards, and much more besides.

"Yes, I did," I said, and my reply was echoed around the group.

Sir Gordon beamed. "Fantastic! Thank you for the feedback. I'm sure this course will be very successful in the future for all who attend. I'll have feedback forms sent out in the week to get your more in depth responses." He clapped his hands together. "Wonderful!"

"Sorry, but, don't you think a murder might put people off? Or attract more people like Fergus?" I added.

"Hey!" Fergus protested.

Sir Gordon smiled benevolently. "Well, I'm not sure that there is any such thing as bad publicity. Although, what happened here was tragic, no doubt." He lowered his voice so that any nearby police wouldn't hear. "Almost as tragic as what befell the young man with big dreams that I once employed to redesign my garden several years ago. It was his first project you know." He looked seriously at me for a moment, and I realised that either someone had told him that I'd figured out the truth, or perhaps he was just guessing and saying something that would make no sense to someone with no idea. I shot him a knowing look and he seemed satisfied.

At least now I had my answer. Sir Gordon had given a young man a chance. He'd seen Elliot's potential before anyone else and then he'd seen that potential taken from him. I understood why Sir Gordon and the others had sought a kind of justice that would otherwise have eluded them.

Moments later we were dismissed by the police, but advised to stay contactable in the probable case of further questions. Everyone had played the part they'd hoped to play all along.

I sincerely doubted that the police would ever find the mysterious intruder who had murdered Christine Montague over a few pieces of jewellery. The only person who might have been able to understand such a petty and greed-driven motivation was the one lying dead in her room.

Life returned to normal remarkably quickly after the strange few days spent away. I found myself appreciating having the option to contact other people and being able to find out what was in the news, but I still wasn't actually tempted to become more sociable. The time spent with the people on the course had been intense enough for me to not want to see people again for a very long time.

Dogs were a different matter.

Diggory had been very happy to see me when I'd picked him up. His doggy grin had only faded when I'd been told about all of the trouble he'd got up to whilst Fergus and I had been away.

With the autumn colours slowly giving way to Christmas greens, my mind was firmly focused on what I could do to expand my business. Most of my work came from the flyers I'd handed out and posted around the village, and from word of mouth. A few people found my website and there were more who saw me at the market and booked me for events, but beyond those profitable occasions, I spent a lot of time twiddling my thumbs. Big events were great for the books, but they came with a lot of stress and the need to always be answering to the commissioner's desires - just as we'd been taught on the flower arranging course. I realised that if I wanted my business to really bloom, I needed to add something more. Something that wasn't always dictated by the client.

I thought I had just the idea.

I often found that I was left with surplus flowers that didn't always suit the event organiser's tastes. A lot of the other flowers I grew I took to the markets I attended, but in all honesty, that was a lot of hard work. Something about the flower arranging course had inspired me, and it was in the days that followed that I came up with the idea of the subscription bouquet service. Every week I had a whole bunch of flowers that were beautiful, but homeless. If I offered bouquets at a reasonable price and with free delivery... it could just catch on!

I relied on florists for some of my income, as I supplied them with flowers, but I could also see the benefits of cutting out the middle man. For around half the price of a florist, I worked out I could post flowers for people to arrange themselves. With my flower arranging course learned skills, I could also include some tips on how to arrange the bouquets that arrived in the little boxes I'd already found online. I was so excited by the idea, I'd called up Fergus and asked him to come over, so that I could share the news with someone.

The doorbell shook me out of my focused mood, where I had been costing and considering the maximum number of potential subscriptions that my plot of land could sustain. I walked to the door and welcomed a bedraggled Fergus and Barkimedes into my house. The autumnal sunshine had finally turned to a more seasonal wet patch and my guests had been caught in a shower. I gave them both towels and Fergus borrowed my dressing gown. Once we were settled, and I was still getting used to the idea of Fergus in a purple sheep covered dressing gown, I told him about my idea.

"It sounds great! How are you going to get the word out?" he asked immediately after I'd finished.

"Well… I was going to use flyers and put the word out at my market stall. It's more convenient for people. It will be easy to cancel, too. I need to get my website modified so that it can take orders."

"What about a newsletter?"

"A newsletter?" I said, thinking of a piece of printed paper - the kind of thing that was usually shared around a village and contained mostly gossip and the odd lost cat advert.

"Yes, you send it online," Fergus said, shooting me a disbelieving look. He'd known exactly what I'd been thinking of. "It makes getting in touch with you easy and people get to know the real you."

"You think that's a good idea?"

"Sure! It worked for me with The Truth Beneath. My readers love me!"

"Really?!" I said and received a withering look for my squeak of surprise.

Fergus threw his hands up and reached for a biscuit. "Good luck selling your bouquets! Just telling you what I know."

I grinned. "Stop being a grump. For a man who is tongue in cheek about most of what he does, you can't take a joke."

"Oh yeah? You're not so great at good humour either. Or gratitude, for that matter. You were hardly grateful for that fancy course we just went on, and yet here you are, using some of the ideas for your business. Tell me I'm wrong!"

"You're not wrong," I conceded. The course had definitely stuck with me, as Sir Gordon had intended when he'd designed it. The only thing I wasn't certain of was whether the sudden death had been the catalyst for not being able to forget, or the course itself.

I hoped that Sir Gordon didn't aim to have a murder every time he ran the course.

"But Fergus… please… never do anything thoughtful for me again." I was actually half-serious. Where Fergus was involved, trouble seemed to follow very closely behind.

My friend nodded like he was actually taking it into consideration. "But it was fun, right? We saw signs of alien life! I count that as a success."

"You're seriously sticking to your story? I gave you a whole number of logical explanations!"

Fergus grinned. "But you didn't prove any of them, did you? And you didn't disprove that it was, in fact, an alien spaceship answering my call."

I rolled my eyes so far back I was surprised they didn't disappear into my head. "You know the difference between proving something and disproving something! I've explained this before."

"And you'll have to explain it again. Multiple times. I am on a search for the truth, Diana, and I'm going to find it." He might have looked dramatic had there not been half a chocolate bourbon biscuit caught in his stubble. "But, just to clarify… you did learn a lot on that course, didn't you?"

"Yes," I repeated.

"So it was useful. And Fergus is a great friend for taking you," he said, looking self-satisfied.

"Fergus needs to quit talking about himself in the third person, but it was useful." I kept my smile to myself, thrilled that he'd walked into my trap. "So useful, in fact, that I decided to return the favour. I've enrolled you on a course I think you'll like... and I'm coming, too! It's going to be such fun."

"What kind of course?" I was rewarded with Fergus looking every bit as suspicious as I'd been when he'd first announced we were going on the retreat.

"It's just a one day course, so no lockdowns," I hastily told him. I wouldn't be willingly signing up for anything like that again. "It's a conspiracy theory course."

"That sounds vague." Fergus wasn't having the wool pulled over his eyes for a second.

I let my grin escape. "It really is a conspiracy theory course! It's run by a man who specialises in scientifically debunking theories. We'll be learning about conspiracies that have been debunked, and the best methods to investigate and debunk any theory we come across. Sounds pretty fun, right?"

"That sounds like the opposite of fun. This scientist guy must not be open-minded at all."

"Tut, tut! You're the close-minded one. Ever since we met, I've been telling you that you need to find evidence to support your theories. This will be a great chance for you to see how that's done. And engage in a healthy debate," I told him primly.

"But... science is for killjoys!"

I raised an eyebrow. "Are you telling me that you're not interested in finding holes in the argument of a scientist whose goal in life is to debunk all conspiracy theories?"

Fergus looked thoughtful for the first time. "Confronting the enemy! When you put it like that..." He rubbed his chin. I could almost see his brain working. I sincerely hoped that this scientist would be prepared for someone like Fergus.

To be honest, I wasn't sure if anyone was prepared for someone like Fergus.

Diggory reached a paw up for a biscuit, but I neatly pushed it away from the plate. Fergus followed suit and I automatically repeated the action.

"This guy will have to have answered every angle in his debunking. It's easier to prove something exists but difficult to prove that it doesn't. I can be a tricky customer!"

I turned away so that he wouldn't see my smile. "I don't think anyone will argue with you on that point."

BOOKS IN THE SERIES

A REVIEW IS WORTH ITS WEIGHT IN GOLD!

I really hope you enjoyed reading this story. I was wondering if you could spare a couple of moments to rate and review this book? As an indie author, one of the best ways you can help support my dream of being an author is to leave me a review on your favourite online book store, or even tell your friends.

Reviews help other readers, just like you, to take a chance on a new writer!

Thank you!
Ruby Loren

ALSO BY RUBY LOREN

MADIGAN AMOS ZOO MYSTERIES

Penguins and Mortal Peril

The Silence of the Snakes

Murder is a Monkey's Game

Lions and the Living Dead

The Peacock's Poison

A Memory for Murder

Whales and a Watery Grave

Chameleons and a Corpse

Foxes and Fatal Attraction

Monday's Murderer

Prequel: Parrots and Payback

THE WITCHES OF WORMWOOD MYSTERIES

Mandrake and a Murder

Vervain and a Victim

Feverfew and False Friends

Agrimony and Accusations

Belladonna and a Body

Prequel: Hemlock and Hedge

HOLLY WINTER MYSTERIES

Snowed in with Death

A Fatal Frost

Murder Beneath the Mistletoe

Winter's Last Victim

EMILY HAVERSSON OLD HOUSE MYSTERIES

The Lavender of Larch Hall

The Leaves of Llewellyn Keep

The Snow of Severly Castle

The Frost of Friston Manor

The Heart of Heathley House

HAYLEY ARGENT HORSE MYSTERIES

The Swallow's Storm

The Starling's Summer

The Falcon's Frost

The Waxwing's Winter

JANUARY CHEVALIER SUPERNATURAL MYSTERIES

Death's Dark Horse

Death's Hexed Hobnobs

Death's Endless Enchanter

Death's Ethereal Enemy

Death's Last Laugh

Prequel: Death's Reckless Reaper

BLOOMING SERIES

Blooming

Abscission

Frost-Bitten

Blossoming

Flowering

Fruition

Vincent van Gogh

Vincent van Gogh (Dutch, 1853–1890)
Still Life with Apples, Pears, Lemons and Grapes, 1887
Oil on canvas, 46.5 x 55.2 cm (18⅜ x 22 in.)
Gift of Kate L. Brewster, 1949.215

BOX 6099, ROHNERT PARK, CA 94927

Pomegranate

Vincent van Gogh

Vincent van Gogh (Dutch, 1853–1890)
Flowerpiece and Fruit, 1888
Oil on canvas, 54.6 x 44.5 cm (21½ x 17½ in.)
BF#928, Gallery II

Pomegranate

BOX 6099, ROHNERT PARK, CA 94927

Vincent van Gogh

Vincent van Gogh (Dutch, 1853–1890)
Farmhouse in Provence, 1888
Oil on canvas, 46.1 x 60.9 cm (18⅛ x 24 in.)

Pomegranate

BOX 6099, ROHNERT PARK, CA 94927

National Gallery of Art, Washington
Ailsa Mellon Bruce Collection 1970.17.34

Vincent van Gogh

Vincent van Gogh (Dutch, 1853–1890)
Haystacks in Provence, 1888
Oil on canvas, 73 x 92.5 cm (23¾ x 36⁷⁄₁₆ in.)
Rijksmuseum Kroeller-Mueller, Otterlo

BOX 6099, ROHNERT PARK, CA 94927

Pomegranate

Vincent van Gogh

Vincent van Gogh (Dutch, 1853–1890)
Fishing in Spring, 1886/87
Oil on canvas, 50.5 x 60 cm (20¼ x 24 in.)
Gift of Charles Deering McCormick, Brooks McCormick, and Roger
McCormick, 1965.1169

BOX 6099, ROHNERT PARK, CA 94927

Pomegranate

Vincent van Gogh

Vincent van Gogh (Dutch, 1853–1890)
Houses and Figure, 1890
Oil on canvas, 50.8 x 38 cm (20 x 15 in.)
BF#136, Gallery VIII

Pomegranate

BOX 6099, ROHNERT PARK, CA 94927

Vincent van Gogh

Vincent van Gogh (Dutch, 1853–1890)
Girl in White, 1890
Oil on linen, 66.7 x 45.8 cm (26¼ x 18 in.)

BOX 6099, ROHNERT PARK, CA 94927

Pomegranate

Vincent van Gogh

Vincent van Gogh (Dutch, 1853–1890)
The Plains at Auvers, 1890
Oil on canvas, 50 x 101 cm (19¹¹⁄₁₆ x 39¾ in.)
Neue Galerie, Vienna

BOX 6099, ROHNERT PARK, CA 94927

Pomegranate

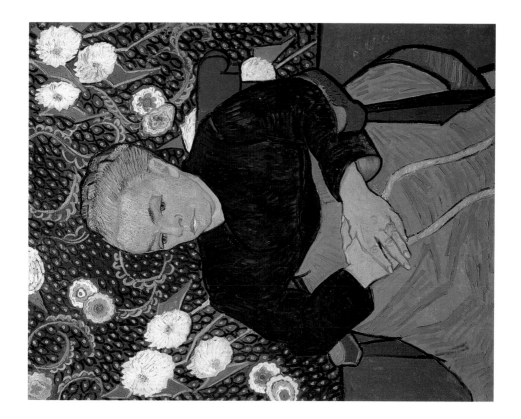

Vincent van Gogh

Vincent van Gogh (Dutch, 1853–1890)
Madame Roulin Rocking the Cradle (La Berceuse), 1889
Oil on canvas, 92.7 x 73.8 cm (37 x 29½ in.)
Helen Birch Bartlett Memorial Collection, 1926.200

Vincent van Gogh

Vincent van Gogh (Dutch, 1853–1890)
Postman, 1889
Oil on canvas, 66 x 55 cm (26 x 21⅝ in.)
BF#37, Gallery II

BOX 6099, ROHNERT PARK, CA 94927

Pomegranate

Vincent van Gogh

Vincent van Gogh (Dutch, 1853–1890)
La Mousmé, 1888
Oil on canvas, 73.3 x 60.3 cm (28⅞ x 23¾ in.)

BOX 6099, ROHNERT PARK, CA 94927

Pomegranate

National Gallery of Art, Washington
Chester Dale Collection 1963.10.151

Vincent van Gogh

Vincent van Gogh (Dutch, 1853–1890)
Landscape with Carriage and Train in the Background, 1890
Oil on canvas, 72 x 90 cm (28⅜ x 35⅞ in.)
Pushkin Museum of Fine Arts, Moscow

BOX 6099, ROHNERT PARK, CA 94927

Pomegranate

Vincent van Gogh

Vincent van Gogh (Dutch, 1853–1890)
Self-Portrait, 1886/87
Oil on artist's board mounted on cradled panel, 41 x 32.5 cm (16⅛ x 13 in.)
Joseph Winterbotham Collection, 1954.326

BOX 6099, ROHNERT PARK, CA 94927

Pomegranate

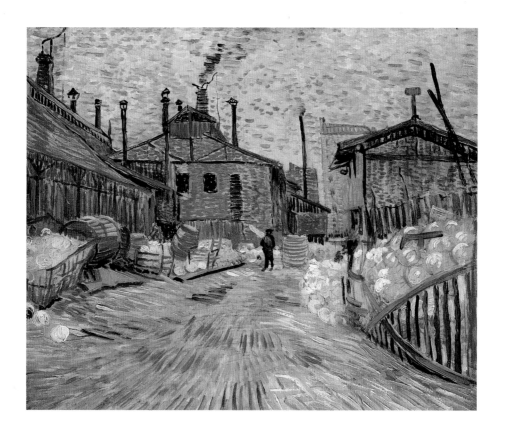

Vincent van Gogh

Vincent van Gogh (Dutch, 1853–1890)
Factories, 1887
Oil on canvas, 44.1 x 54 cm (17⅜ x 21¼ in.)
BF#303, Gallery VI

BOX 6099, ROHNERT PARK, CA 94927

Pomegranate

Vincent van Gogh

Vincent van Gogh (Dutch, 1853–1890)
The Olive Orchard, 1889
Oil on canvas, 73 x 92.1 cm (28¾ x 36¼ in.)

BOX 6099, ROHNERT PARK, CA 94927

Pomegranate

Vincent van Gogh

Vincent van Gogh (Dutch, 1853–1890)
The Garden of the Asylum in Saint Remy, 1889
Oil on canvas, 73.1 x 92.6 cm (28¾ x 36⁷⁄₁₆ in.)
Folkwang Museum, Essen

BOX 6099, ROHNERT PARK, CA 94927

Pomegranate

Vincent van Gogh

Vincent van Gogh (Dutch, 1853–1890)
A Peasant Woman Digging in Front of Her Cottage, 1883/85
Oil on canvas, 31.3 x 42 cm (12½ x 16¾ in.)
Bequest of Dr. John J. Ireland, 1968.92

BOX 6099, ROHNERT PARK, CA 94927

Pomegranate

Vincent van Gogh

Vincent van Gogh (Dutch, 1853–1890)
Man Smoking, 1888
Oil on canvas, 62 x 46.4 cm (24¾ x 18¾ in.)
BF#119, Gallery XIII

BOX 6099, ROHNERT PARK, CA 94927

Pomegranate

Vincent van Gogh

Vincent van Gogh (Dutch, 1853–1890)
Roulin's Baby, 1888
Oil on canvas, 35 x 23.9 cm (13¾ x 9⅜ in.)

Pomegranate

BOX 6099, ROHNERT PARK, CA 94927

Vincent van Gogh

Vincent van Gogh (Dutch, 1853–1890)
The Red Vineyard, 1888
Oil on canvas, 73 x 91 (28¾ x 35¹³⁄₁₆ in.)
Pushkin Museum of Fine Arts, Moscow

BOX 6099, ROHNERT PARK, CA 94927

Pomegranate

Vincent van Gogh

Vincent van Gogh (Dutch, 1853–1890)
Still Life: Vase with Irises, 1890
Oil on canvas, 92 x 73.5 cm (36¼ x 29⅜ in.)
Rijksmuseum Vincent van Gogh, Amsterdam

Pomegranate

BOX 6099, ROHNERT PARK, CA 94927

Vincent van Gogh

Vincent van Gogh (Dutch, 1853–1890)
Montmartre, 1886–87
Oil on canvas, 43.6 x 33 cm (17⁷⁄₁₆ x 13¼ in.)
Helen Birch Bartlett Memorial Collection, 1926.202

Vincent van Gogh

Vincent van Gogh (Dutch, 1853–1890)
Lupanar: Tavern Scene, n.d.
Oil on canvas, 39.3 x 31.2 cm (15½ x 12¼ in.)
BF#104, Gallery XIV

BOX 6099, ROHNERT PARK, CA 94927

Pomegranate

Vincent van Gogh

Vincent van Gogh (Dutch, 1853–1890)
Mlle. Gachet in Her Garden at Auvers-sur-Oise, 1890
Oil on canvas, 46 x 55.5 cm (18⅛ x 22¼ in.)
Musée d'Orsay, Paris

BOX 6099, ROHNERT PARK, CA 94927

Pomegranate

Vincent van Gogh

Vincent van Gogh (Dutch, 1853–1890)
La Meridienne (after Millet), 1890
Oil on canvas, 73 x 91 cm (29¼ x 36⅛ in.)
Musée d'Orsay, Paris

Pomegranate

BOX 6099, ROHNERT PARK, CA 94927

Vincent van Gogh

Vincent van Gogh (Dutch, 1853–1890)
Seascape at Saintes-Maries, 1888
Oil on canvas, 44 x 53 cm (17⅜ x 21¼ in.)
Pushkin Museum of Fine Arts, Moscow

Pomegranate BOX 6099, ROHNERT PARK, CA 94927

Vincent van Gogh

Vincent van Gogh (Dutch, 1853–1890)
The Bedroom, 1889
Oil on canvas, 73.6 x 92.3 cm (29⁷⁄₁₆ x 37 in.)
Helen Birch Bartlett Memorial Collection, 1926.417

Pomegranate

BOX 6099, ROHNERT PARK, CA 94927

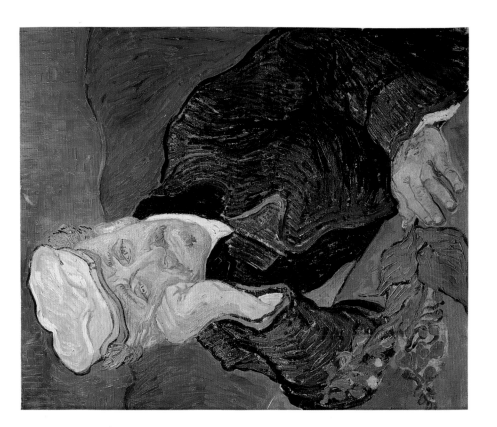

Vincent van Gogh

Vincent van Gogh (Dutch, 1853–1890)
Portrait of Dr. Gachet, 1890
Oil on canvas, 68 x 57 cm (27¼ x 22¹³⁄₁₆ in.)
Musée d'Orsay, Paris

BOX 6099, ROHNERT PARK, CA 94927

Pomegranate

Vincent van Gogh

Vincent van Gogh (Dutch, 1853–1890)
The Drinkers, 1890
Oil on canvas, 59.4 x 73.4 cm (23¾ x 29⅜ in.)
The Joseph Winterbotham Collection, 1953.178

BOX 6099, ROHNERT PARK, CA 94927

Pomegranate

Vincent van Gogh

Vincent van Gogh (Dutch, 1853–1890)
Memory of the Garden at Etten, 1888
Oil on canvas, 73.5 x 92.5 cm (29⅛ x 37 in.)
L'Hermitage, St. Petersburg

Pomegranate   BOX 6099, ROHNERT PARK, CA 94927